Genetic Heroes

Written by:
Christopher Stamper Sr.
and
Mike McCarron

Cadmus Publishing
www.cadmuspublishing.com

The authors invite any and all fans and readers to write your thoughts
and comments. How to reach the authors. (Address envelopes as illustrated
below.)
(Author)
Christopher Stamper Sr. 20895-035
Federal Correctional Institution La Tuna
Post Office Box 3000
Anthony, NM 88021

(Co-author)
Michael McCarron 19907-023
Federal Correctional Institution La Tuna
Post Office Box 3000
Anthony, NM 88021

CONTENTS

CHAPTER ONE

I wake up at 6:30 am to get ready for school. As I head out the door mom and dad said, "Have a good day." I walk in to school.

I hear my friends say "Hey Chris, over here." I walk over to my best friend Jacob; we're both 16 years old and sophomores in high school.

I ask, "Where are Sammy and Tiffinie? They're usually here before us?"

Jacob said, "I'm not sure."

I said, "After school we get to pack up for spring break and leave for the cruise ship in the morning."

As I feel hands go over my eyes and I hear, "Guess who?"

I spin around and pick Tiffinie up and she laughs. I put her down.

She asks, "Can I ride with you to the cruise ship?"

I said, "Yes, all four of us are riding together."

Tiffinie said, "Great."

As the school day ended, we were walking out of school and

Travis yells, "Hey, stupid", as he trips me. He pushes me to the ground with his friends kicking and beating me. Travis loves to bully people. I went home.

I said, "Thank god for spring break!" I went to pack my bags, then got a shower and went to eat supper.

As mom and dad ask, "Are you ready for the trip?"

I said, "Yes, sir. Yes, ma'am."

I go lay down and I get a text from Tiffinie saying, "Hi, what are you doing?"

I said, "I'm laying down in my room."

She said, "Ok, good night."

I said, "Good night."

Then I planned the trip as I plan the routes. I put it in my GPS on my phone and I lay back and relax. I get down and pray before I fall asleep as I start to dream. I dream about Tiffinie and me. She is telling me "She likes me." As we kiss for the first time on the ship in our room.

She says "I have always liked you and I want us to be together." She is laying in my arms with her head on my chest.

I asked, "Are you sure?"

She smiles and says, "I always have."

The next morning there's a knock on the door and mom opens the door.

Tiffinie says, "Good morning Mrs. Stamper."

Mom says, "You can go get Chris up."

She smiles and says, "Ok."

I hear, "Wake up, sleepy head."

I opened my eyes. I see Tiffinie.

I say, "I'm still dreaming," and close my eyes.

She laughs and blushes. "No, you're not, get up! We've got to get going."

I get up. She goes and puts her stuff in the truck as Jacob and Sammy gets dropped off.

As I come up the stairs, mom and dad hug me and say, "Be

safe."

I say, "Love y'all, bye." I step outside.

Tiff yells, "I got shotgun," and she gets in the front seat.

Jacob and Sammy get in the back seat. I get in, shut the door and put a dip in. I pull out of my driveway and head south.

Tiff looks at me and asks, "So, you're dreaming about me," and she giggles.

I asked, "Do you want a real answer to that?"

She says, "Yes, I do."

I said, Well, then, you already know the answer."

She says, "Yes, I do, but say it."

I say, "Ok. I dreamt about you."

She blushes and Sammy said, "Awww."

Sammy said, "You guys are so cute together."

Tiff said, "We ain't together."

Sammy said, "Too late. I see how you guys look at each other."

Tiff said, "We do not," then she looks at me and blushes.

Sammy said, "See!"

Tiff says, "Shut up."

Sammy laughs, so do I.

Jacob said, "Women!" I laugh.

We pull over and get gas. Jacob went inside for drinks and snacks. Sammy says, "Chris, please don't hurt my friend. She has always liked you."

We load back up. We hit the highway as it gets dark Tiffinie falls asleep and her head winds up on my shoulder.

Sammy whispers and says, "She really is in love with you Chris."

I ask, "How long?"

"Since she first met you."

I said, "The same for me."

She said, "So cute," and then said, "Goodnight, Chris," and fell asleep on Jacob.

So, I drove through the night to make time and get to the ship.

Tiff moves then starts talking in her sleep and I smile. I hear her say, "Really, Chris?" then mumble and start breathing heavy again.

As the sun comes up, we drive to the top of the next hill. I see the coastline of Florida. Tiff wakes up and sees the same.

She says, Sorry I fell asleep on you."

I smile and say "It's ok. You're beautiful when you're asleep."

She blushes and smiles as we pull into the parking lot down by the docks. We park by a red Honda Element. Jacob and Sammy get out.

I grab Tiff's bag as we unload and carry them to the ship. We see three men dressed like they work on a cruise ship. Orater says to his two friends, "See, easy grab and go. We can rob them all blind and be off the ship before it leaves."

I pull out our tickets. The guy checks them.

He called, "Chris Stamper, Tiffinie Hale, Jacob Snodgrass and Sammy Heart," as we boarded.

They show us to our rooms; me and Tiff in one, Jake and Sammy in the other. Tiff went to get a shower. I went and laid down. I fell asleep. Tiff smiles when she sees me asleep. She lays down beside me and watches tv.

I wake up to Tiff saying, "Wake up, Chris."

She was in her two-piece swimsuit. She smiles.

"Jacob and Sammy are waiting for us to go swimming."

I put on my swimming trunks. We walk to the pool as Tiff and Sammy sat sun bathing. I tell Jacob to watch this I swim up to Tiff. I touch her legs. She runs her finger across my forehead to push my hair aside.

I then pull her into the water as she comes up, I take her in my arms and she laughs. I use my fingers to brush her long brown hair out of her face. I look into her brownish-green eyes. She smiles shyly and asks, "Who are they?" I look up and see two 16-year-olds standing by the pool looking at us. One man, one woman.

The man laughs and asks, "Do you recognize me?" The woman smiles at the question.

He said, "We have history class together. My name is Mike Smith and this is my girlfriend, Linnea Michelson."

I said, "I'm Chris. This is Tiffinie. Right there is Jacob and Sammy."

Tiffinie asked, "Do y'all want to have dinner with us tonight?"

Linnea smiled and said, "Yes," then asked, "Who is that guy over there?"

Sammy said, "He looks like a creep. I see his name tag; it says Orator."

Jacob says, "See you guys at dinner."

Him and Sammy left as we got out of the pool.

Tiff says, "See y'all at dinner."

As we walk together, they said, "See you guys at dinner."

We got our showers, we put on casual clothes, and I tell Tiff she looks beautiful in her green dress. As I pull Tiff's chair out and she sits I sit beside her. As Jacob, Sammy, Mike and Linnea came in and sat down.

Tiff asked, "How did you meet Mike?"

Linnea said, "We met at a rock concert. It was a local band."

Also, "How long have y'all been together?"

She said, "Two years."

Then Linnea asked, "How long have you and Chris been together and how did you guys meet?"

Tiff looked at me and blushed and said, "We're not a couple. We met in elementary school."

Linnea said, "Oh, sorry. I just thought."

Tiff smiles, "It's ok."

Linnea asked Sammy the same questions.

Sammy said, "We all four met in elementary."

She said, "Me and Jacob just started dating."

I look at Tiff. She looked sad, so I took her hand and she smiled.

Mike asks, "What's everyone's plan on doing when they grow up?"

I said, "Military."

Tiff said, "College, to be a nurse."

Jacob said, "A chef."

Sammy said, "A housewife."

Linnea said, "Beautician."

Mike said, "I want to be a computer repair tech."

We ate and talked a while, then Tiff said, "I'm tired."

I said, "Ok."

I told everyone goodnight. We walked back to our room. We laid down. She turned over. I could hear her sniff like she was crying. I touched her.

I ask, "What's wrong?"

She says, "Nothing." I turn her face to me. I wipe the tears from her eyes as she lays her head on my chest and sobs.

She then asks, "What's wrong with me?"

I say, "Nothing, why?"

"Then why don't you like me?"

I said, "I don't like you, Tiff. I'm in love with you, but I'm nervous. I don't want to mess anything up.

She said, "How can you? We're all we know. I have always loved you from the beginning. Hang on, I will show you how much I love you." She looked at me. She went to get up. I looked into her eyes and kissed her. She smiled and said, "Hold that thought." She got up and took her shirt and pants off.

She gets back into bed and smiles and says, "I want you to be my first and I want to be your first tonight."

I couldn't take my eyes off of her as she looked at me with love in her eyes. We kiss as all of a sudden, we're thrown off of the bed. We laugh, but then I hear crew arguing with each other. As I take Tiff in my arms as we get thrown into the wall, I keep her safe.

I was bleeding. I told her to get dressed. So, did I. We went to

Jacob and Sammy's room. I told Tiff to stay as I ran out and went up to the pilot house. I see the Captain.

I ask, "What's going on?"

He says, "A hurricane is pushing us off course." As winds and waves hit us, he said, "Y'all get somewhere safe." I run back to Jacob's room as we all meet in the hallway. As the ship rocks and tosses us around, I yell, "It's not safe in here, too much debris."

I grab Tiff by the hand as the lights went out. We ran to the pilot house. Jacob, Sammy, Mike and Linnea followed as we crossed into the Bermuda Triangle. Crew and people vanished as we made it to the pilot house.

Orator turns as he is talking to his friends to say, "Next time, don't take so damn long." As he turns, his friends vanished. He takes off to find them as he says, "Those damn fools."

Tiff said, "Chris, you're bleeding badly. Sit!"

Sammy ran and got a first aid kit. Tiff put pressure on it and she cleaned me up as the Captain came in to see six kids in the pilot house.

He asked, "Where is my crew?" as he checked gauges and they read empty and no power.

I said, "Your crew vanished."

The compass is spinning as a woman walks in. He smiles and says, "My name is Captain John Tonaka and this beautiful woman is my friend, Chloe Addams." We all introduce ourselves. We look up and the ship is headed towards land as it comes into fast view.

Captain Tonaka yells, "Brace for impact, now!"

I grab Tiff and hold her against the wall. The ship hit land and me and Tiff went flying through the window of the ship with my body going through first. As Tiff stayed wrapped in my arms as I hit the deck and I black out.

I hear Tiff crying, "Please wake up."

I open my eyes. She hugs me. She kisses me. I sit up. I see Sammy, Chloe and Linnea.

I ask, "Where is everyone?"

Tiff said, "Getting supplies and exploring."

I get up. Tiff said, "Move slowly." I see four men coming from the woods.

I ask, "Who's the fourth guy?"

Sammy said "That creepy, bald, no teeth guy."

So, we sat there as they came up.

Jacob said, "Glad you're up, we found food."

I said, "The ship has food, but let's eat."

We ate and looked around and I started a fire on the beach. It got dark.

I said, "My upper back hurts between my shoulder blades."

Tiff said, "Me too."

I asked, "Did you hit anything? Are you ok?"

She said, "No, I didn't. You took it all for me," as she hugged me.

I said, "I meant it when I said I love you," and she smiled.

We laugh. I said, "I guess no more school."

They said, "No, there's not."

I look at Tiff and ask her to be my girlfriend. She smiles.

"So, you wait until we're stranded to ask me?"

I say, "Yes."

She said, "Chris, my answer is I love you. Of course, yes." I kiss her.

Sammy said, "About time, you guys."

Tiff blushes and laughs. So, we all tell stories of our past. We joke and laugh.

I said, "We will be ok and make it through this and make it home."

Tiff said "Let's all get some rest. It's been a long day."

I look at Tiff. I said, "You feel like you're in love."

She blushes and says, "I am with you," as we go into the ship and to our rooms.

As we lay down and cuddle up, I tell her, "I'm glad I didn't lose you."

She smiles, I kiss her goodnight, and we fall asleep.

CHAPTER TWO

Two years later, the phone rings. Mom answers and a man asks, "Is this the Stamper residence?"

Mom said, "Yes, this is Becky Stamper."

The man said, "Ma'am, I'm calling on behalf of your son."

She asked, "What has he done now? I'm sorry officer, he's been like this since his brother died."

The man said, "Ma'am, I'm not an officer, I'm a doctor. I'm calling because you need to come down to Four City Memorial Hospital. Your son, Chris Stamper, has been found and you need to get here."

Mom asks, "Is he dead?"

He said, "No, he's alive along with a few others."

Mom dropped the phone then she told everyone. They got everyone in the car as they headed that way. Mom and dad were standing there looking through the door.

The doctor looks at them and says, "He's healthy. He has some tests that came back strange. Also, x-rays were strange along with all the scars not from the shipwreck."

Doc said, "Look, he's not going to be the same as he was before. Also, don't separate him and Tiffinie. They can't be away from each other. We tried. Just keep them together. Also, the other six can be separated from them, but they have to be not too far away." They opened the door. I turned and looked as I smiled and hugged mom and dad.

**

Then Tiff's mom and dad comes in and they hug her then they left to talk. They discussed, outside with my parents, what the doctor was saying. Tiff's dad said, "I don't care. We're taking our daughter home."

Tiff came and hugged me. She said, "I love you," then our parents came in together and said, "Let's go home, Tiff."

As Tyler took her and guided her out of the door, mom and dad came in and guided me out as we step outside the news media surrounded us. As we pushed ourselves through, we made it to the car and headed home. We get home. I go to my room as I feel the need to be with Tiff.

**

Linnea and Mike's parents come in as Linnea cries and hugs her parents. Everyone is smiling.

Mike's dad asked, "What happened?"

Mike replied, " I guess we were in a wreck."

Mike asked, "Dad, how is everyone?"

He said, "We're all fine and we're happy that you two are not dead."

The doctor told them not to separate Mike and Linnea, also don't be too far from the other six.

They asked, "Why?"

He said, "I don't know. We tried here. Just do what I said until I can run more tests. The tests came back strange. So, please do as I say."

They separated them and took them home to their own houses and they felt it, too.

**

I waited until I heard everyone in the house was asleep and I slipped out of the window. I ran to the park. I saw Tiff. She saw me and ran and jumped into my arms. I kiss Tiffinie, then I hear Jacob say, "You guys go get a room."

Mike said, "Yeah, you two should."

Linnea and Sammy laugh. I said, "Maybe we will."

Then Captain John Tonaka and Chloe Addams show up. Then our parents pull up and walk over to us. Tiff started to cry as Tyler and Karla came up with my mom and dad.

Tiff cried, "I can't be away from him! I need him and he needs me, please!"

All six of our parents were talking as I got down on one knee and asked, "Will you marry me?"

Tiffinie was crying and smiling and said, "Yes," as we kissed.

I see everyone staring and then clapping as I hear mom, dad, Mr. and Mrs. Hale say, "Their eyes are a bright green."

I put an engagement ring on her finger as they walk up.

Mom and dad say, "You two are staying with us tonight."

The others are going to stay close around as we all went home. Tiff climbed into bed with me. I tell her let's move to the floor as I fall asleep on the floor she stays in bed. Mom and dad come in as it's storming outside. They see me tossing and turning.

Mom touches me and says, "It's ok. It's just a bad dream."

I jump up, open my wings and flip her and dad stops me from breaking her neck. I back into the corner of the room. Tiff comes over to me and says, "It's ok," as she holds me, she says, "I'm safe, so is everyone else."

Mom and dad says, "No, they need to stay together, they need each other," as they left me and Tiff fell asleep on the floor.

I wake up to Tiff laying with her head on my chest. I run my fingers through her hair. She opens her eyes and they're bright green.

She smiles and asks, "How are you?"

I said, "Better."

She said, "It's my parents' house tonight after school."

I said, "Ok."

Mom comes in and says "Y'all get up, time to go to school", and hands me a shirt that was custom made for my wings.

We come out of the room. Mom said, "Come home, then y'all go to Tiff's house."

I say, "Ok. I love y'all," and head to school.

All six of us meet at the door of the school. We spend the whole day in another world. At lunch time, I see the army recruiters. I fill out an enlistment form and signed it. They smile as I leave the cafeteria. We leave school. As Travis sneaks around and follows Chris and tries to stay right behind him to fight him. I see we're being followed as I pull up at my house. Me and Tiff went to get some clothes.

    **

During school, Mike spent the day in a whole other world. The teachers talked and talked, but none of it registered. Linnea, noticing Mike's attitude, said, "Earth to Mike."

Mike replied, "Huh, oh hey!"

Linnea asked, "You okay?"

"Yeah," Mike said, "You work it out where I can stay with you?"

Linnea said, "Yep."

School passed by and then Linnea and Mike left for Linnea's house. Spaced out they never noticed being followed.

    **

I look as we pull out of my driveway and go to Tiff's house. A car follows us to Tiff's house. I pull in the driveway. Tyler let us in and hugged Tiff.

Then he said, "Chris, you sleep in the guest room."

As I lay in the guestroom, I hear people snoring in the house. I jump up when I hear my door open. As Tiff comes in and lays beside me.

I get a feeling to come to the park, so me and Tiff leave and we go to Raven City Park. All eight of us meet at the park. We were all standing there. I showed them my wings. Then, out of nowhere, Tiff opened hers. Mine were solid black. Hers were solid white.

Travis sees their wings, so he videos and says, "What the hell. I can't believe this."

We were standing there when vehicles came in at every direction. Everyone took off in one direction. They get out with guns. As they shot, I pushed Tiff to take off as we ran. As she got in the air, I jumped in front of their shot and I rolled. I can hear Tiff scream. She went to come back for me but they loaded me up. Jacob and Mike grabbed Tiff.

They told her, "We can't help him!"

She screams, "I can't feel him! He's dead!"

Jacob said, "He's strong," as Tiff cries "I need him!"

**

Running along the streets as fast as they could, the remaining group dodged in and out of streets and alleys.

Mike, panting and out of breath, asked, "What just happened? Where do we go?"

Linnea said, "I know of an abandoned warehouse close by."

So, they ran, following Linnea to the warehouse. Still unsure about being followed, they entered the building. Stopping and catching their breath, they all stared out in shock.

Tiff's hysterical sobs punctuated Sammy and Jacob's reassurances. Afraid of being followed, John said, "We really need to be quiet right now."

This earned him some glares as Linnea set to work at finding better hiding.

Linnea said, "I don't like this! Who were they?"

Mike replied, "I don't know, but they were well armed."

Chloe, joining Linnea's efforts, found a dark back office. Sammy and Jacob helped Tiff to this office.

Mike said, "I'll keep a look out."

Linnea instinctively joined him.

Before leaving, he said, "If we yell, run!"

Jacob said, "Ok" as Sammy reassured Tiff "Chris is ok."

Tiff just rolled up into a ball and cried herself to sleep. As Jacob was watching out a window so was Sammy.

Jacob said, "I saw Chris go down after being shot protecting Tiff."

Sammy said, "I know, I can't feel him either, but neither can she."

Jacob said, "We have to find him. She won't go without him. Let's take the night."

Jacob spent all night trying to figure it out with Sammy asleep.

CHAPTER THREE

I wake up to see a man and three women. I try to move, but I can't. I see my arms and legs are strapped down.

The man says, "Mr. Stamper, do you know who I am?"

I said, "No, sir."

He said, "I am President John Moris. The three women here; this is General Samantha Wilson, Commander Chelsy Moris, and your doctor, Lieutenant Holly Bass. I know all about you and that you want to be in the military."

I said, "Yes sir, I did."

He said, "Alright, I will make a deal with you. I will make you a Captain and in full command of universe labs."

I asked, "What's the catch?"

He said, "All of you have to live here and no one can know you're super human."

I asked, "What about family?"

He said, "Only on leave and come to visit. I know they know, if they don't keep it that way."

I said, "Yes sir, it's a deal."

They all agreed and Lt. Bass unstrapped me.

Lt. Bass said, "Sir, here is your uniform and gear, it's custom made for your wings."

I said, "Thank you."

She shows me around. I see my office and everything. I get on my uniform and gear and I fly out. I can feel Tiffinie as I fly and search. I can feel the air on my face. I can feel I'm getting close. I see an old abandoned warehouse. I land on top.

I climb in a broken window. I work my way down the back stairs. As I open the door to the first floor, I shut the door quietly and walk down the hall. I find a dark office and go in. Because of my eyesight, I can see Tiff clearly. I run my fingers through her hair and kiss her. She opens her eyes. Tiff screams and jumps in my arms and kisses me.

**

Mika and Linnea were staring out the front door. Mike's eyes start to droop as a snore escapes out of Linnea.

Mike shook awake and said, "What's the point?" then went back to watching.

Just as Mike was about asleep, a feminine scream ripped through the night. Mike and Linnea woke with a start. They yelled at the same time, "The office!" Running back to the office, Mike and Linnea burst through the door.

**

Mike, Linnea, John, Chloe, Jacob and Sammy all coming into the office to see Tiff in the arms of a soldier. I put Tiff down and turn around they are looking at me shocked. I tell them everything. Mike and everyone agreed to come with me. Humvees pull up and we all get in a few hours later we pull into the vehicle bay. Lt. Bass came in as we get out. She showed everyone to their apartments.

Every couple shares an apartment.

Lt. Bass says, "Captain Stamper, all of y'all have two days off to settle in. Have a good day, sir."

We unpack then sit down and cuddle up on the couch and watch TV together.

Tiff asked, "How soon can we get married?"

I ask, "How does tomorrow sound?"

Tiff smiles, "Yes, I want to."

Tiff texts everyone and tells them the news. Sammy knocks on the door.

Sammy comes in and tells Tiff to "Come on, we have a lot to do before tomorrow."

They leave. I go into mine and Tiff's room and get a shower. I go to my new office when there is a knock at the door. Lt. Bass comes in. I get a dip.

She asks, "Sir, what are you doing here?"

I said, "One: call me Chris when it's just us."

She said, "Call me Holly."

Then I said, "Tiff is planning our wedding for tomorrow."

She said, "Congratulations."

I said, "After the weekend we will get to work."

Holly smiles and leaves. I sit back and look around and say "This will be hard, but we can do it. At least we're at peace and we're all safe." Then I see Orator is a new congressman and moving up fast.

**

Meanwhile, in Mike and Linnea's apartment, Linnea was relaxing on the couch and watching TV. Mike was bustling about unpacking and setting up the place.

Mike asked, "You need anything, babe?"

She replied, "Water, please?"

As Mike gets a bottle of water, a text comes through their phones announcing the wedding.

"Heck yeah!" Mike said to no one in particular. Then, to Linnea, "We're going, right?"

Linnea replied, "Uh, yeah."

Linnea got up and started getting things ready for the next

day. Mike flopped on the couch. They spent the rest of the night settling in and getting ready.

**

I go home and lay down. I fall asleep. The next morning, Jacob wakes me up and says it's time to get ready. I get my Class A uniform on as everyone else was already there. John is going to do the ceremony. I'm standing there with my best man. The bride's maids on the other side with everyone else in their seats. Then the music plays as Tiffinie walks down the aisle.

I can see her smile as I take her hand.

I say, "You look beautiful."

I see tears rolling down her face. As the ceremony went on, Pastor John asked, "Tiffinie, do you take Chris Stamper as your lawfully wedded husband?"

Tiffinie said, "I do."

Then John asked, "Chris, do you take Tiffinie Hale as your lawfully wedded wife?"

I said, "I do."

Then John said, "With the power vested in me, I pronounce you husband and wife. You may kiss the bride."

I lift her veil and kiss her tenderly as everyone clapped. As we left hand-in-hand, we went to the reception and we prayed. Then the best man said a toast. We ate. Then me and Tiff had our first dance.

Lt. Bass asked Tiff if she could cut in and congratulations.

Tiff said "sure" as she went and danced with her three friends.

Holly said, "Congrats."

I said, "Thank you," as we danced.

She said, "I know you're not worrying about the next couple of days, but we sent DNA samples from all of y'all to Hamilton Labs."

I said, "Ok, when?"

She said, "This morning."

I said, "Ok, it's fine."

She smiles as I spin her around. Tiff comes back and Holly leaves. I pull Tiff in close and kiss her.

Tiff and her friends are sitting at the table laughing, while me, Mike, Jacob and John are standing by the bar watching them. I get a dip.

Jacob said, "We're all grown and on our own now."

I said, "Yeah."

Jacob smiled and said, "It's about time you started a life with her."

I said, "Yes, she's the one, my true soulmate. What about y'all three. It's y'alls turn?"

Jacob said, "Soon I will marry Sammy."

Mike said, "Heck yeah! I'm going to marry Linnea!"

I laugh and say, "Good," then John said, "Well I ain't getting any younger and Chloe is an amazing woman."

Tiff waves at me and smiles. I wink at her.

I say, "Our whole worlds have changed. I wonder if it's for the better. Everything feels right."

Linnea comes and takes Mike to the dance floor, then the other three come and get us. I pull Tiff close as we dance. I spin her around. She puts her arms around my neck.

Tiff said, "Your body feels stronger and you have muscle."

I said, "Yes, I changed like you did, babe."

Tiff said, "I have a surprise for you tonight." I smile. She said, "You're my husband and I'm ready."

I said, "Let's enjoy our wedding and tonight I'm all yours."

She said, "Deal."

We went and sat down and watched everyone have fun.

Tiff says, "I'm a lucky woman."

I said, "I'm a lucky man. Look at my wife and our friends."

Tiff smiles, "You're right, we're both lucky," as she lays her head on my shoulder.

As the reception died down and as everyone left, they congratulated us. We walked back to our apartment. I open the door then pick her up and carry her across the threshold. I shut the door with my foot then I carry her to our bedroom.

She smiles. "I will be back," she says. "Linnea caught the bouquet."

I laugh and say "Mike is next."

CHAPTER FOUR

Tiff goes in the bathroom and comes out in green lingerie. She smiles. I go kiss her. I pick her up and lay her on the bed. I kissed her down her body. Then we made love for the first time ever, as we connected. She had an arrow form on the left side of her chest. It's just like mine over my heart and both of ours are glowing red.

As we became one, the little white things coming from our sexual organs connect and intertwine together. We can see, feel, hear, know, everything about each other, our thoughts, memories. We know what each other wants and needs (even sexually). As we finish making love, the little white things go back in us. You can't tell from the outside what happened.

Tiff lays with her head on my chest, our naked bodies against each other's, as she smiles.

She says, "That was amazing."

I say, "Yes, it was."

She gets up. I watch her.

She says, "I'm going to get a shower."

I get up. She smiles and her bare feet dancing down the hall. She's running her fingers down the wall. She dances around in just my t-shirt.

She says, "Come get me if you can," so I chase her into the bathroom and into the shower and I take my shirt off of her.

As the water runs, we make love again. We get cleaned up. She puts my shirt back on.

She asks, "Are you hungry?"

I say, "Yes," and she goes and cooks.

She hands me my can of dip and then kisses me. She brings me supper and we eat. Then she cleans up. She walks by and I pull her into my lap and kiss her. Then we head to bed. She cuddles up to me as she falls asleep.

I whisper, "I love you! Goodnight my beautiful bride."

I lay awake and finally start to drift off to sleep.
**

Mike and Linnea arrive at their apartment, joking and laughing. The bouquet still in Linnea's tight grip.

"You caught that thing like a receiver catches a football," Mike said.

"You liked that?" Linnea replied, smiling ear to ear.

Mike said, "Of course. But who are you going to marry???" a wolfish grin on his lips.

Giggling, Linnea said, "Stop it."

Settling onto the couch, Mike suddenly became serious.

Mike said, "Everything is changing, isn't it?"

She settled next to him. With a sigh, she said, "Yes. Yes, it is."

"I have only this," Mike started, gesturing around, "And the future is completely uncertain, but will you marry me, my love?"

Crying, Linnea said, "Yes, oh yes!"

Sealing the promise with a kiss, they finished the night cuddling and watching TV.
**

My phone rang. I answer "Captain Stamper."

I hear, "Captain, it's Lt. Bass. You're needed."

I said, "Alright." I get up and put my uniform on. It's black digital ACUs. Then I put my gear on. Tiff wakes up. I kiss her.

She said, "Be safe."

I say, "I love you."

She said, "I love you too." I head down to the conference room as Lt. Bass lets me in.

I hear, "Good morning, Captain Stamper."

I said, "Good morning, General Wilson."

General Wilson said, "The alarms went off at Hamilton Labs, no one has reported in."

She said, "Captain, I want you to take a unit and personally check it out."

I said, "Yes, ma'am."

Lt. Bass comes in and says, "Sir, your unit is ready and I'm assigned to it."

I said, "No doc, you're needed here."

She went to refuse, but she got mad. We loaded up and she watched the tail lights of the Humvees. Holly went to talk to Tiff in tears. Holly knocked on the door. Tiff came to the door in my t-shirt.

Tiff asked, "What's wrong Lt. Bass?"

She said, "Captain Stamper wouldn't let me go on this assignment. I can't protect him."

Tiff said, "It's ok, he will be fine. You won't lose your Captain. I won't lose my husband." Tiff saw it in her eyes.

We pull up at Hamilton Labs. We get out and breach the front doors. I feel alone and hungry, but why? As we enter, the lights are flickering. I hear a baby cry. I sent the unit in pairs to search. I breach the lab. We search there were dead mutants. I see a baby alive. She has blonde hair and bright green eyes.

I pick her up. She has two knots on her back like me and Tiff. As I carry her, they look at me.

I say, "I hear movement outside."

I call the rest of the unit in.

I said, "I heard something outside, be on alert."

Prv looked at me, he asked, "Are you sure Captain? I don't hear anything."

I say, "Yes. We need to stack up at the entrance."

They yell "Yes, sir", as they sit waiting to move out.

We moved out. I didn't see anything. As we started to get in the Humvees, shots rang out. The soldier beside me hit the ground dead. I pulled my sidearm and shot two as my men fired back.

As my entire unit fell, I shot more. I hear someone yell, "Medic!" as the radio hit giving our coordinates. Ambush Delta 4 down soldier's down. I was hit. I fell against the Humvee with the baby in my arms. I fire back then I was shot several more times. I hear, "Captain down," as I feel being dragged. The Private saw how bad I was.

The Private said, "Captain Fly get the baby to safety."

I spit blood. "I'm not leaving my men."

He said. "They are all dead."

Then he was shot in the head and two of my fingers were shot off. I opened my wings and flew off as I poured blood, struggling to keep flight.

**

Tiff and Holly were talking. Then Tiff said, "I feel alone and hungry, but I just ate and so did Chris." As Tiff asked, "You like Chris?"

Holly said, "Honestly, yes I do but he's your husband."

Tiff said, "I'm not threatened or scared, I'm connected to him," as Tiff started to scream,

Holly asked, "What's wrong?"

Tiff said, "Chris is hurt bad," as Holly got the call "Delta 4 down Captain Stamper and his unit are down."

Holly left in a hurry.

Tiff yelled, "He's still alive, but hurt badly."

**

My vision is getting blurry as I bleed out. I fight to stay up in the air and use what's left of my strength. I land in front of the vehicle bay by the cameras. I stand against the wall. I slid down the wall as blood smeared down the wall. I cradle the baby as I sit in a puddle of blood.

**

The alarm sounded in Universe Labs as Lt. Bass ran outside with a team of medical professionals. Holly saw Chris on the ground sitting against the wall. They lay him on a stretcher. He has a baby, so we take them both in. As they cut and take everything off, Tiff and everyone was sitting outside waiting. I open my eyes and whisper, "Name the baby Karley," as I pass out then I flatlined.

Lt. Bass came out with the baby she said, "Mrs. Stamper, the baby is a girl and she is yours and Captain Stamper's biological daughter."

Then tears came in her eyes and said, "He wants her named Karley."

"How is Chris?" asked Tiff.

Holly said, "He had an aneurism, he didn't make it."

Tiff said, "Let me see him," as tears streamed down her face. So did Holly.

Holly said, "I'm sorry, I can't," as they all cried.

Tiff said, "I can save him."

Tiff cries and gets sick. Holly does a check up on her and says, "You're pregnant."

**

Mom and dad were in the kitchen when there was a knock on the door. There were two uniforms and mom's heart stopped. Mom dropped to her knees as dad helped her up as Lt. Bass handed them the letter. As they left, mom read the letter from me in case I died. The news told the story of the ambush on Captain Stamper and his unit were all killed.

**

Holly went to her apartment. She opened the letter I left for her. It said, "Dear Holly, I know you like me. I need you to let Tiffinie come near me and don't tell people I'm dead. Please, do this for me. One last time. I know it's breaking protocol." Holly went to talk to Tiff and everyone was in Tiff's apartment. Holly asked them all to come and they walked back to the infirmary.

CHAPTER FIVE

Mike and Linnea stood a polite distance back from Tiff. Linnea cried quietly. Mike stood stoically. His mind was afire with anger.

"Those mother truckers who did this to them and who made that baby," Mike thought over and over.

Quiet anger and revenge on his mind, Mike tried to convince himself that if he was there, things would have been different. Mike knew the truth; nothing could fix it.

"The world is full of crazy. I need to stay ahead of it," Mike thought.

As the group started to leave, following Lt. Bass, Mike shook himself back to reality. "Time to deal with this new reality," he thought.

**

Lt. Bass let Tiffinie and Karley in. They looked at the sheet that covered Chris' body. Tiff went and flipped the sheet and uncovered Chris' face. Tiff saw Chris she started to cry. She kissed his cheek and touched his face. Holly turned pale when the body started to breathe again. Holly removed the sheet to uncover all of the gunshot wounds healing.

Lt. Bass called all of the medical staff to the infirmary as they came in hooked him up to machines.

One said, "He's been dead for hours."

They try to make Tiff leave, but Lt. Bass said, "It's an order. She stays."

They moved Chris to recovery. Tiff sits by the bed and holds Karley and holds my hand. Lt. Bass comes in to do a workup on Chris. As Mike and Linnea come in, they offer to take Karley for a while so Tiff can be with Chris.

Tiff said, "Thank you."

Linnea said, "I love babies."

A few hours go by. I open my eyes. I see Tiff with Karley. Tiff smiles at me then calls for Lt. Bass.

Tiff says, "I have two surprises for you," as she cries and hugs me.

Tiff said, "I thought you were dead."

I said, "You saved me," and she kisses me. I smile.

Lt. Bass comes in and checks vitals.

She smiles and says, "Welcome back, Captain."

I said, "Thank you," and she leaves.

Tiff says, "One, Karley is our biological daughter, and I'm also pregnant."

I smile and kiss her. She hands Karley to me as she looks at me and smiles.

Everyone comes in to see me. We talk for a while. They all go. When visits over, Tiff takes Karley home and puts her to bed. Holly comes in.

She said, "I didn't ever think I would be able to ask you; how did you know I like you?"

I said, "It's clear as day."

Then Holly said, "Tiffinie isn't worried about it."

I said, "No, because we can't connect to a normal human."

Holly asked, "What?"

I said, "We have one mate for life. We can have intercourse with humans."

I tell her about the connection part. She smiles.

I say, "We can't connect to humans, so we can't become one or have babies with humans." I said, "That's why."

She said, "Well then, I'm no challenge to her at all." Holly said, "Well you have two women who are in love with you. You have one more night in here."

Then she hands me my can of dip. Then says, "I didn't give that to you." She smiles and leaves as I get a dip and watch TV and relax as I sit there waiting for tomorrow.

**

Mike and Linnea sat in their apartment with the TV on for background noise. Mike was in a mood.

Linnea asked, "Babe, what's wrong?"

Mike replied, "Now how do we get revenge?"

Linnea said, "We leave that to the military."

Mike sighed. "You're right. Again. How was holding the baby?"

"It was nice. I can't wait to have one of our own."

Mike said, "We need to marry soon. Today taught us that. Think the ladies would help plan it?"

Linnea said, "Oh babe, yeah. I hope they will." Linnea texted the ladies and waited for a reply before going to bed.

**

Holly comes in to check on me and her phone rings so she said, "I got a text from Linnea. Linnea asked if we would help her plan Mike's and Linnea's wedding."

Holly texted said, "Of course I will."

Tiff texted, "Of course I'm in."

Sammy texted "Me too."

Chloe said, "Me too."

Holly told me everyone is in and they asked Linnea when do

you want to start planning? Also, when is the wedding?
**

Linnea, on receiving everyone's texts, said, "It's really happening. When do we want to have it?"

Mike replied, "Of course, it's happening. We're a team and we rock. How about next week? Say Saturday?"

Linnea smiled. "Okay, that sounds right. Linnea Smith. I like that. Team Smith."

Linnea stared off dreamily. Linnea texted, "Let's start planning tomorrow and the wedding is next week on Saturday."
**

I said, "Good."

Holly said, "You go home tomorrow. Goodnight, Chris."

As I lay down and go to sleep, Holly wakes me up the next morning and releases me from the hospital. So, I walk back to the apartment. Tiff and Karley are already gone. Tiff left a note saying she went to Linnea with her friends and Karley planning the wedding.

I lay down on the couch to relax as I look around board. So, I get up and go to the lab to work out.

Dr. Kayla comes in and asks, "Should you be doing that?"

I said, "I'm healed, just hook me up."

So, she did. As I warmed up, then I used the salmon ladder, then I flew a few laps. Then I ran a few laps, I worked out on a punching bag, then I started training with a compound bow. I went to reach for an arrow when it floated into my hand and shot.

Dr. More came in and said, "That was awesome, Captain!"

I said, "Yes, it was," as she took the monitors off.

A few days has passed. It's Thursday. I wake up. I smell coffee and get up. I walk out and see Tiffinie cooking breakfast in panties and my t-shirt. She was dancing around the kitchen as I walked in. Karley is in a high chair. She giggles and screams, "Daddy!" Tiff turns around and smiles and says, "Good morning, baby."

I kiss Karley on the head and tell her, "Good morning."

She giggles and says, "Morn daddy."

I go hug and kiss Tiffinie.

I say, "I love you and Karley is growing fast. She looks three."

I look at Tiff she looks six months pregnant.

I ask, "How's my beautiful glowing wife feel this morning?"

Tiff blushes and says, "Eat, then we'll get dressed. I'm going to Linnea's today to help finish up on the wedding plans for Saturday."

I smile and say, "I will take Karley with me today."

Tiff asks, "Are you sure?"

I said, "Of course, we need time together."

Tiff asks, "How is Dr. More working out?"

"She's a good doctor until Lt. Bass is done helping with the wedding."

Tiff said, "We have become good friends," and she kisses me and says, "Thank you."

She gets Karley dressed and herself as I got dressed and put my gear on. I kiss Tiff.

I say, "I love you, you look beautiful, have a good day."

She leaves with a smile.

I look at Karley and the diaper bag and say, "It's just us."

She looks at me. I pick her up as I open the door Prv Tillten was there.

He said, "Good morning, Captain Stamper. You're needed in the conference room. Commander Moris is waiting, sir."

I walk in and salute Commander Moris.

She said, "Good morning, Captain. Any new information on Hamilton Labs?"

I said, "No ma'am, all scientists and doctors were gone. We don't know what happened to them, who ambushed my unit, or how Karley was created with mine and my wife's DNA."

She asks, "Is that Karley?"

I say, "Yes, ma'am."

She says, "Aww, she's a cutie. When you find anything Captain, you report it to me."

I say, "Yes, ma'am."

As the day went on and we headed home we gave Karley a bath then her little wings came out, white with black tips. We feed her, put her to bed, then we go and get a shower. She wears nothing but my t-shirt. We cuddle up and go to sleep. A couple of days has passed. It's Saturday morning the morning of Mike and Linnea's wedding.

As we sit in the chow hall, we wait as our families come in and sit with us. We all laugh and joke. I see everyone having a good time. I smile as I see everything feels so right. Our families hug us, then they head out to go back home.

Chapter Six

The day of the wedding dawned, bright and sunny. Mike and Linnea awoke excited and ready at the same time. Mike got up, drank an energy drink, and began seeing to getting ready. Linnea got up and messaged Holly that she was ready to get ready. Holly messaged back that she was ready as well.

Linnea left to Holly's apartment. Mike went to the chapel and checked on last minute decorations as everyone started to arrive. Mike greeted everyone as the bride's maids and the best man took their place. Then he took his place at the altar. Captain Tonaka officiated the ceremony.

Music played. Linnea came down the aisle on her dad's arm and she stood in front of Mike. Heartfelt vows were exchanged. "I do's" were said to many tears. Finally, John said, "You may kiss the bride!" The kiss exchanged was chaste and appropriate.

The reception was small and for close friends. Good food was served, along with tasty drink. An awkward dance followed by a hasty retreat by the bridge and groom.

The bride and groom spent the night passionately consummating their marriage. On consummation, a symbol that looked like a tsunami appeared on Linnea's chest.

Mike whispered, "I love you, my love."

"I love you, too," Linnea whispered back.

They fell asleep in each other's arms, ending a perfect day.
**

Me and Tiff walked into our apartment with Karley asleep in my arms. I take and lay her in her bed. Me and my beautiful wife sit down and cuddle up on the couch.

Tiff said, "That was a beautiful wedding."

As we fell asleep together on the couch with the TV on. We wake up. Karley was standing in her crib as we walked in.

Tiff says, "I got her."

Tiff gives Karley a bath. I get a shower in our bedroom bathroom. I get my uniform and gear on. I walk into the kitchen and kiss Tiff as she cooks breakfast. Tiff kisses me and hands me a cup of coffee.

Tiff asked, "What's your plan for today?"

I said, "Work," as a broadcast came on the news.

President Moris came on and made a statement that he was stepping down and so is the Vice President. He announces the new President is Orator. There was a knock on the door.

Tiff answers the door and I hear, "Good morning, Mrs. Stamper."

I hear, "Good morning, Lt. Bass," as they hugged.

Lt. Bass asks, "Where is Captain Stamper?"

Tiff lets her in. Lt. Bass says, "Good morning, Captain."

I said, "Good morning. Why so formal?"

She said, "We have to meet with the new President."

I said, "Alright."

I kiss Tiff and tell her that I love her. Then, I kiss Karley on the head.

I tell her "Be good for mommy," as Tiff hands me my can of

dip.

Me and Holly left for the conference room.

Lt. Bass said, "The President is waiting in the conference room," as we walk in, I say "Mr. President."

He shakes my hand and says, "Captain Stamper."

Then he asks, "You're in command of Universe Labs, right?"

I say, "Yes, sir."

We give him a tour of the facility.

He says, "This place is amazing and results are amazing. How would you like a promotion and I want to reward you the Silver Star for saving that baby at Hamilton Labs."

I said, "I will take command of Hamilton Labs, but I want to stay a Captain."

He said, "No problem, Captain."

I say, "Mr. President, I don't want the medal, either. This operation needs to stay a secret. People can't know about us."

The President looks at me.

He says, "That's why you're in command."

I said, "I got a cleanup crew headed to secure Hamilton Labs right now."

President looks at Lt. Bass. "How would you like a promotion?"

Lt. Bass asks, "What's it, intel?"

He said, "You're going to Hamilton Labs under Captain Stamper's command."

Lt. Bass said, "All due respect, sir, I'm Captain Stamper's doctor. I can't leave him. This is my life's research."

He looks at me and says, "I will let you staff and control Hamilton Labs, it's under your command."

He shakes our hand and leaves.

Holly looks at me and says, "He's a strange guy."

I said, "He's super human."

She laughs. "So are you, but I like you."

I said, "He tried to control your mind, but I intervened."

She smiles. Says, "So you're my hero and you knew what I

wanted to say?"

I said, "I'm not sure."

She hugs me and says, "You did and I want to stay your doctor and friend and see where this goes."

As she leaves, she says, "Thank you."

I go to my office. When my phone rings, I answer, "Universe Labs, Captain Stamper."

I hear, "Captain, please listen to me now, get everyone out of Hamilton and Universe Labs."

I ask, "Who is this, and why?"

The voice said, "Captain, you need to move now! President Orator is sending the full U.S. military to kill all of you guys."

I run to the intercom system and tell everyone to pack up and get to the vehicle bay now. As I run to my apartment and get what we need and grabbed Karley and her stuff. I have Tiffinie texting everyone. I hit my radio and set soldiers by every entrance.

**

Mike and Linnea started their day late. Mike kissed Linnea and went to get an energy drink. At that moment, the intercom goes off for evacuation.

"What the heck is going on? Better do what he says," Mike said.

Linnea was already packing when Mike joined her. Quickly, they packed what little they had. Mike chugged his energy drink then grabbed one for the road. Hustling out of the door, Mike and Linnea said goodbye to their apartment. Grabbing the duffel bag and her hand, Mike led the way to the vehicle bay.

**

As the outer perimeter alarm goes off, we pull out and go straight down a hidden path I told everyone to follow me. I hear tanks, Humvees, Bradlees and jets behind us. Thank god for this cover of trees. As we meet up with Hamilton Labs' vehicles and we all convey out. We drove for hours and pull over for a break as soldiers grouped into unit and spread out.

Lt. Bass comes up and asks, "What in the world was that?"

As Tiff, Jacob, Sammy, John, Chloe, Mike, and Linnea come up as I say, "President Orator sent the U.S. military to kill all of us and destroy both labs."

Lt. Bass said, "I got all of our research. Nothing was left behind. How did you know?"

As a text comes in with a picture of the abandoned Quad City military base. The text said, "Here's your new home. Enjoy. Lay low for a while all of you guys."

**

Mike and Linnea finish stretching and climb back into their vehicle. "Quad City?"

Linnea asked. "I know, right? Do you trust our tour guide, the warning voice? I think we have to, right?"

Mike replied, "Yeah, I think we do."

Then Mike pulled out and joined the convoy.

**

As we drive on Tiff takes my hand.

She says, "I'm scared."

I said, "Don't be. I won't let anything happen to you."

My phone rings I answer the voice says, "Captain Stamper."

I say, "Yes, go ahead."

The sign says "Welcome to Fort Quad."

The voice says, "Welcome. Everything is unlocked for you guys. Once you're in I will lockdown the outside."

We drove into the vehicle bay.

CHAPTER SEVEN

Lt. Bass showed everyone the underground military base and their new apartments. I go to my new office then I go to the new labs and work out. I hit the salmon ladder as Tiff and Holly comes in.

Tiff says, "I love when he does that and shirtless."

Holly laughs. "I see why."

Holly walks up to me and hands me a new ACU jacket with an archer hood on it.

It was black digital with an arrow patch on it and a black eye mask. Then my phone rings it's a text saying "We will meet in a few days when things cool off."

I text back and say, "Deal."

I put my uniform and gear on the mannequin as everyone trains and meets with their doctors for test and checkups.

As Dr. Blaine did a checkup on Tiff and said, "In a couple of weeks the baby will be born."

**

Mike and Linnea start to settle into their new apartment when a message comes through Mike's phone. The message read, "Good morning. I am Dr. Cook and at your earliest convenience I would like to see you and Linnea."

Mike replies, "In an hour sound fine to you?" after consulting Linnea.

Dr. Cook messaged back, "Sure."

They spent the hour unpacking and resting. The doctor met Mike and Linnea in a large room. He introduced himself and explained the tests. Dr. Cook wanted to see what Mike could do. By throwing objects at him, Dr. Cook forced Mike to control the air around them to deflect them.

**

Tiff and I went home and unpacked and gave Karley a bath. As we lay in bed, Tiff traces my hand and puts it on her stomach as the baby kicks.

So, I started talking to Tiff's stomach I say, "This is your daddy. Please be a boy, I need help with your mom and sister."

Tiff laughs and says, "We're not that bad and you love us."

I say, "I do love you both with all of my heart, but I'm outnumbered."

**

Mike's tests went on for a few hours. Each object thrown getting easier to deflect. Finally, Dr. Cook ran some bloodwork and vitals. Linnea had bloodwork and vitals taken. Then they went back to their apartment.

Back in the apartment, Linnea exclaimed, "What was that?"

"I guess I really am an airhead," Mike replied.

Mike pulled Linnea in for a kiss and a hug.

Mike said, "I love you no matter what happens."

Mike and Linnea settled in to the new couch and watched TV. The last thing Mike said before falling asleep was, "This changes everything. We need to prepare for changes."

**

I woke up to my head by Tiff's stomach and Tiff's fingers

running through my hair.

Tiff says, "You fell asleep talking to the baby."

I get up and get a shower. Tiff goes to cook breakfast and gets Karley ready for the day. We eat and I head to the lab to train. Holly comes in with the full medical reports for all nine of us. She told me all of their abilities and genetics and their health.

I said, "Well, I will try telekinesis."

Holly said, "You have been using it to shoot arrows and you didn't even know."

I said, "Ok," and went to train with just telekinesis. I learned to teleport and a few other things. I got a text that says, "Meet me in the vehicle bay."

As I gathered the units all throughout the vehicle bay and every entrance. As me and Lt. Bass stand beside me as the door unlocks and opens.

**

Dr. Cook wakes Linnea up by messaging "Your turn" to her. Mike and Linnea head back to the same room. This time, a sensor was added to the object throwing.

"Just go invisible, Linnea, and you won't get hit," Doctor Cook explained.

"Invisible?" Mike asked.

After a few tries, Linnea was turning invisible and staying that way for longer and longer.

"Holy guacamole," Mike yelled at first. After a few hours, Mike and Linnea went back to the apartment.

**

Two vehicles pull in as Arial, Tommy, Alis, Allana, Tyson, Hanna, Skyler and Ella all get out. Arial comes up and hands me a phone all of their moms and dads were on the phone.

They told me, "The government is onto the eight of them for protecting y'all. We all agree for them to be with y'all and safe also for them to work and to become heroes like you. We want them to enlist with you we know y'all are fighting against the evil of the cities, government, injustice.”

"We all agree for you to train them so they can help you they are being followed by the government.”

I have Lt. Bass take them and put them in the apartments with their families.

As I go to my office and Arial comes in, she says, “It was me who you were talking to.”

She shows me. She says, “I had to protect you your family.”

I hug her and I get a dip and she goes back to the apartment. As. Lt. Bass and I work on a game plan.

**

I go to the lab with Lt. Bass as she says, “Let’s send you to Raven City.”

She said, “I will call you Captain Arrow. That’s your code name.”

I put my uniform on. I pull my hood up. Holly smiles as I put my gear on. I go outside as the sun sets. I open my wings and fly off. I sit on the edge of a building.

I hear in my right ear Arial say, “Hay Cap, I’m with you.”

I say, “Ari.” She interrupts and says, “Captain, it’s Bird Watch and yes Lt put me here. Plus, give me a chance. I saved you so let me help. Plus, when you fly in, we have a new roof entrance for you.”

I hear a scream. I look down. I see a man grab a woman. I fly down and land in the alley.

As I walk, I hear the man say, “Scream, no one can hear you!”

I say, “I can.”

He looks at me and gets off of her and he says, “Get out of here! Who do you think you are?”

As he pulls a gun I pull and shoot an arrow through his hand. As he screams then I shoot an arrow through his chest. I help her up. I turn to leave.

She yells, “Thank you,” as I open my wings and fly off. I watch from the rooftop as the blue lights fill the alley. I see a gas station and change clothes then I go in. I get a Coke, some snacks and a can of dip, then go outside.

**

Mike was sitting with Dr. Cook at that moment.

Mike said, "So, let me see if I got this right. I can manipulate air, perform telekinesis, and I regenerate slowly. Plus, my wife can turn invisible."

Cook just said, "Yup."

Mike replied, "That is awesome! Does this mean I'm a super hero?"

Cook sighed, slightly bored with the situation. "Yes, we want you to take care of Waveport City. You are code name Tsunami."

Mike said, "Do I get a theme song?" Then, in a whisper, "It's important."

Cook said. "We don't provide theme music. Can you be serious about this?"

Mike frowned. "Maybe. We shall see."

CHAPTER EIGHT

I see a blonde woman walk into the gas station and I see her buy some stuff and talk to the cashier. I see the blonde point at me they laugh. She starts to leave. So, I started to leave.

I hear behind me, "Sir, I need to talk to you."

I turn. I say, "Yes, ma'am? You're a Detective, right?"

She asks, "How do you know?"

I say, "Your gun and normal clothes."

She said, "Yes, but I'm not being a Detective now. I just never seen you around here before."

I look at her and say, "I'm Chris."

She says, "I'm Juliet."

I said, "Nice to meet you, but I have to get to work."

She smiles and hands me her card to call her.

I said, "Ok, I will."

She asks, "Will you meet me here tomorrow at the same time?"

I said, "We will see."

She turns around. I disappear.

I sit on the ledge of a building as Juliet turns around to see me gone. I see her get in her car as I pull my hood up and over my head. I hear, "Captain."

I said, "Yes, Bird Watch."

She says, "You're on the news already."

I said, "Good, I'm headed in."

She says, "Ok, Cap."

I fly. As I get close, I see a door open on the roof so I fly in and land on the floor.

**

Mike walks into his apartment, excited to find Linnea on the couch crying.

Mike said, "What happened?"

Linnea said, "Hunter died today."

Mike said, "Oh baby, I'm so sorry. What can I do?"

Linnea cried. "Nothing, but be here for me."

Mike wrapped his arms around Linnea and held her. Inside, his anger seethed, but he dared not show it. Tomorrow, Mike would get to work, but today he was Linnea's. As they laid down to sleep, fitful rest settled upon them. Mike and Linnea dreamt of death in very different ways.

**

I look up and see a command center. Arial looks up and Lt. Bass comes up to me smiling as I put my hood down.

Holly says, "It's all over the news. You saved the Mayor's and the Detective's youngest sister. Well, they don't know it was you, they said a hooded man saved her life."

I said, "I did what is right."

"Arial said they are looking for the vigilante."

I tell everyone, "Good job today," and I went to go get me a shower.

We eat supper. Tiff looks at me and says it's time. I look at her as she is sweating and in pain by the look of her face. I call Lt. Bass and Dr. Blane and we met them at the hospital in the base.

**

Linnea was dreaming. She knew she was. It was of Hunter still alive and well. Linnea was the one dying, taking her place. Over and over, she found ways to take Hunter's place. Over and over, it didn't fix anything. Sweat formed on her brow.

Mike was also dreaming. Friends and relatives stood around him. One by one, they turned blue and fell. First mom, then dad.

Each stared into his eyes and said, "You did this. You caused this."

As they fell, a gravestone popped up with the epitaph of "Mike did this." And so, Mike and Linnea tossed and turned in their sleep.

**

As I stand by Tiff as she pushes, I hear Lt. Bass say, "Push one last time."

She does, then we hear the baby cry. Dr. Blane says it's a boy congratulations as he hands the baby to Tiff. She smiles.

Tiff says, "Look at his wings." Solid black with white tips. I kiss her and tell her I'm proud of her.

She says, "I'm tired."

Tiff says, "His name is the same as his daddy's. He's a junior."

**

Mike wakes early the next morning and gets to work designing his costume. All blue, with white pinstripe suit. Then he designs a luchador mask that is dark blue with white waves going over the eyes.

Mike then takes the design to Dr. Cook and Dr. Lake, saying, "I want this and I want to kick some ass. And soon."

**

The next morning, Lt. Bass calls me, Jacob, John, and Mike in to the lab.

She said, "First, this is not the lab anymore. It's the command center. Also, y'all have partners. Captain Arrow, Hanna Addams is Emerald Arrow. Red Web, Skyler Michelson is Shadow. Captain Cross, Tyson Addams is Tribulation. Ok now, Blue Hurricane,

Tommy Hale is Water Spout."

I tell Lt. Bass, "Me, Jacob, John and Mike can go out tonight not with partners until they are trained."

**

Mike pulls Tommy aside and says, "Let's start training."

Tommy says, "Lets."

Mike and Tommy start with basic dodges and blocks. Then, slowly move into basic hand-to-hand training.

Two hours later, sweat dripping from their brows, they shake hands.

"That was pretty good," Mike says.

Panting slightly, Tommy replies, "Yeah, it was. Same time tomorrow?"

Mike says, "Definitely."

**

I show Hanna what to do and we all come together to start training. I show Hanna how to use a bow. She misses so I show her. She says it's easy for you, you're not using a real bow. So, I take hers and do the same.

I said, "It takes discipline."

I ask Holly to take over as I got my uniform and gear on. So did Mike, Jacob and John.

I open my wings and say, "Stay safe. Contact me if y'all need back up."

Jacob said, "Alright," as I flew up through the new door and out into the night sky. I land on the top of a building next to the gas station. I change as Detective Nielson pulled up. I flew down.

**

Mike puts on his newly tailored gear and requisitions a car with a police scanner. Getting in, he tunes to the frequency of Waveport City. Driving off towards the city, he thinks, "Now, someone will pay for the evil in the world." As Mike arrives at Waveport, a call comes in about a robbery in progress. Speeding to a block shy of the location, Mike uses his air control to float himself to the rooftops and over to the building. Sneaking down to the floor with the robbers, he sends a couple of controlled blasts of air and knocks them out. Finally, he sneaks away as the cops arrives.

**

I walk up and say, "Hey Detective."

She spins around and jumps. She sighed and hits me.

Juliet said, "Don't sneak up on me, Chris, and where did you come from? You disappear and reappear."

I tell her, "It's a secret."

She looks at me and whispers, "You were one of the kids that went missing with that cruise ship."

As we sit on the curb by her car, she says, "Sorry, it's none of my business, but nothing was going on in this city until I saw you."

I ask, "What do you mean?"

Juliet looks at me and says, "The vigilante shows up the same day you did."

"So, you think I'm the vigilante?"

She smiles. "Of course not. I don't see any wings."

Arial says, "Captain, we have a location on Billy. He's the governor of Raven City."

As Juliet says, "I have a call."

I said, "Ok."

She smiles. "I will text you."

She pulls out with her lights on. I run, change, then I fly to the address Arial sent me.

**

Mike spends the rest of the night wandering from rooftop to rooftop. The city goes quiet and all seems to fall asleep. At around three am, Mike yawns and decides to call it a night. Mike climbs back into the car and drives back to home base.

Walking into the apartment, he finds Linnea asleep on the couch. Waking her with a kiss, they both climb into bed.

**

I land on the roof of Governor Billy's house. I open a window. I see a light on in the study. So, I listen as Billy talks.

He says, "Sir, we're going to find them."

I hear, "Yes sir, bye."

I walk into his study and shoot an arrow into his hand into the wall as he screams.

I said, "You have failed our city. You had my units set up to be ambushed at Hamilton Labs."

He begged, "Please."

I shoot an arrow through his ear.

I say, "I will be back tomorrow at the same time if you don't step down out of office. Also, tell them why you had my unit ambushed."

He looked at his hand then looked up. I was gone as RCPD showed up. Governor Billy told Detective Nielson everything.

She asked, "Governor Billy, what did you do for him to come after you?"

He said, "That has nothing to do with your job, which is to protect me."

**

Mike awoke the next day after another fitful night sleep. Turning on the TV and tuning into Waveport Channel 4 news, Mike catches a story about the robbers being foiled. Inspired by the news, Mike calls up Tommy Hale.

Mike said, "Ready to train harder? Meet me at the gym."

Tommy says, "You're the boss."

Grabbing an energy drink, Mike dresses for a workout and heads out.

Mike and Tommy begin training with hand-to-hand and slowly evolve into team attacks against sparring partners. Finally, Mike introduces light use of powers. This, combined with Tommy's prowess in martial arts, proved unstoppable … in practice at least.

**

The next day, I get up I have a text message from Juliet saying, "I will text you when we can meet."

I go and train with Hanna for a while. I grab two bamboo sticks, so did she. As we move and the sticks connect and she learns the movement. Then, I change and hit her legs and swiped her legs out from under her. I ask Arial if there was anything on the news about Governor Billy.

She said, "No sir."

I get my uniform on and kiss my family bye and wish the team good luck, then I fly off. As I fold my wings down and dive, I teleport into Governor Billy's study. He looked up.

I said then, "You didn't do the right thing. You have failed my city," as I shot three arrows into his chest.

I teleport to the top of a building close to the Governor's house. I watch Detective Nielson run in the house.

I hear her ask, "How did he get in here?"

I get a text from Juliet saying, "I will meet you anywhere you want to when I get off work in an hour."

I said, "Ok, deal."

Then I hear, "Captain Arrow."

I say, "Yes Bird Watch."

She said, "You're on the news for killing Governor Billy."
**

Mike was just finishing practice when he was approached by a tall, slender female.

Holding out her hand, she said, "Ella Michelson, but you can call me Lighthouse. I'm going to be your eyes in the skies."

Shaking her hand. "Glad to meet you."

Ella reached in her pocket and brought out an earbud.

"With this, I can direct you. No more aimless wandering."

Taking the earbud and putting it on, Mike said, "Early birthday present? Thank you!"

Mike left to shower and change into his gear. Getting ready, he went back to Waveport City. Floating up to a rooftop near downtown, Mike surveyed his city. A salty breeze blew on shore, as the afternoon slowly turned to dusk.

Just then, Mike heard, "Blue Hurricane."

Mike said, "Go ahead, Lighthouse."

"You are up."

CHAPTER NINE

I hear, "Captain Arrow" as I'm flying.

I said, "Yes, Bird Watch,"

"There was a silent alarm that went off at the bank."

I teleport in. I hear police sirens. I see hostages. I start teleporting them out. I get them all out as one of the bank robbers came in and pulls a gun on me as the other two come in. One says, "I have heard about you." The one holding a gun moves towards me.

I shoot an arrow into the gun as he pulled the trigger and it blew up in his hand. It burned his face and metal shrapnel in hand and face. He hit the ground. The other two ran at me and lifted their guns as I shot an arrow into one's chest. I kicked the gun out of the other's hand. As the police came busting in, I teleport out and away. I stand on the top of a building, perching for a few hours.

I get a text from Juliet saying, "I'm headed to a small dinner if you want to meet there."

I text back saying, "Yes."

**

Mike asked, "What do we have?"

Lighthouse replied, "A madman is loose inside a school with a gun."

Ella directed Mike to the school. As Mike arrived, police and SWAT were getting set up. Floating onto a second-floor walkway, Mike gains quick access to the school.

Mike said, "Where is he, Light?"

She replied, "First floor."

Running along, corridor after corridor, Mike's heart was pounding. Turning onto the first-floor hallway, Mike stood face-to-face with the gunman. Amped up, Mike sucked all the air from him, suffocating the gunman. Finally, Mike made a quick escape as SWAT breached the door.

**

I change clothes and go to the dinner and I sit down and wait for Juliet. Five minutes later, she shows up. I greet her then we sit down.

She says, "Sorry, it's been a busy day."

I look at Juliet and say, "Tell me about it."

She says, "The vigilante. There are now four of them."

I asked, "In this city?"

She said, "No, all four cities. We're going to find them and arrest them for murder."

I asked, "Why didn't he save your sister?"

She said, "Yes, but he can't be killing people."

We talk and eat. I pay the bill as we go our separate ways. I teleport home. I take my uniform off. I get in the shower and let the water run over my head. I feel arms go around me. I turn to see Tiff in the shower with me. I smile. I take her in my arms and pull her close and kiss her. I made love to her. We get out get dressed. I walk out to the living room. Karley runs up to me and screams, "Daddy!" I pick her up and hug her.

I kiss her and say, "Bed time."

She giggles and asks, "Daddy, read a bedtime story."

So, I take her and tuck her in. I read her a story about a princess. She falls asleep and Jr is asleep. Then Tiff and I head to bed. Holly sits in her apartment.

She says to herself, "Me and Chris needs more time together."
**

As Mike floats away, he watched police storm the school. Using the local foliage as cover, Mike sneaks away undetected. A block away, Mike touches down on the roof of an apartment building.

Mike heard in his ear, "Well done, Blue. Picture perfect."

Mike said, "Thanks. Now what?"

Light said, "Come on in." Mike said, "Roger."

Mike got back home quietly. Mike went home and changed out of his gear. After getting a shower, Mike joined Linnea on the couch to watch TV.

Mike said, "My love, I love you."

Linnea replied, "I love you too!"

Snuggling, they both finished the night and retired to bed.
**

I get up to Tiff cooking, Karley eating, and Jr is in his swing. I eat and drink coffee and kiss everyone goodbye as I head to my office. I put a dip in as I hear a knock on the door.

Holly comes in and says, "Good morning."

I said, "Good morning."

Holly asks, "Can I hang out with you today in the office?"

I tell her, "Sure, but I'm going out tonight."

She smiles. "I know, you're a hero, even if they are calling you a killer."

I look at her and say, "I am a killer. That's what you have to be to save people."

She says, "No, Chris, you don't have to kill."

I laugh and ask, "Yes, I do, or they keep coming back."

Holly frowns and asks, "Will you try not killing for me?"

I look at her and say, "I will try."

Then she hugs me and says, "Thank you."

Holly asks, "Can I work out and train with you and Hanna?"

I tell her, "Of course you can."

We get up and go to the command center. All three of us train together. I look at Hanna. I tell her go get cleaned up and get into uniform.

Hanna smiles and says, "Yes." I look at her, then say, "You will listen to me out there, Emerald."

We get our uniforms on. Hanna gets on a motorcycle. I open my wings and fly out. I hear Captain we have an amber alert and the cops are on the chase. She gives the vehicle description and location. I tell Emerald Arrow to get in on the chase and be safe as I dive down and see the car. I get a call. I answer.

I hear, "Hey, hon."

I say, "Hey, I'm a little busy."

She asks, "Where is the bottle opener?"

I say, "In the cabinet," as I hear a knock on the door.

I ask, "Who is that?"

She said, "No one," as I land on the car.

**

Mike awakens from a nightmare covered in sweat. Looking at the clock, he decides it's late enough, so he gets up. Mike takes a shower and gets dressed. Mike heads into the gym to find Tommy already there.

Mike says, "Couldn't sleep either?"

Tommy says, "No, too anxious to go out with you."

Mike said, "Glad you're excited."

Tommy looked at Mike quizzically. "What brings you here so early? You're not an early riser."

Mike replied, "Just couldn't sleep."

Mike and Tommy trained for two hours.

After training, Mike said, "Get dressed, you're coming with me."

Mike and Tommy got into their uniforms and went into Waveport.

As they arrived, Mike heard, "Hurricane, we've got a situation brewing at the docks. It looks like a hostage situation."

"On it, Lighthouse."

Mike and tommy speed to the docks.

An eerie silence fell upon the docks as the cops faced the container ship. The approach was littered with containers and crates, allowing Mike and Tommy to approach with stealth. As Mike boarded the ship, he glanced around nervously. Three men with submachine guns stood on the bridge, watching in the cops' direction.

Mike whispered to Tommy, "Silence your pistol, let's take 'em quietly."

Tommy screwed on his silencer. As practiced in training, they took out the three in rapid succession. Next, they began sweeping the bridge. On the bridge, Mike and Tommy found and neutralized four more gun-toting bad guys. We continued to sweep the ship. On the third deck, they found two men guarding a room. After taking out the men, they opened the door to find 15 hostages.

**

Emerald says, "Captain, I'm in position."

I say, "Do it."

She shoots an arrow into the tire. As the car flips, I teleport in and grab the child and teleport out with her safe. The cops stop. They see the car. The cops pull the guy out and arrest him. They point their guns at me as the news shows up and people yell, "Let him go."

Hanna pulled up in front of me. They turned the guns at her. I run grab her and her motorcycle and teleported as they fired. We wind up on the top of my normal building.

Hanna laughed and said, "My motorcycle is up here also." She smiles. "It's beautiful up here."

I said, "Yes, I can look over the city from up here."

I try to call Tiff. There was no answer. I tried multiple times.

Hanna says, "It's quiet tonight, except they're looking for us."

I said, "Let's call it early and sit in the command if we need to go back out."

She says, "Deal."

So, I teleport us back and we sit and listen. I head to my apartment. Tiff was on the couch.

I ask, "Why is Karley still up? Also, why didn't you answer my call?"

She said, "Well, I was busy with the kids."

Karley said, "Daddy, mommy's doctor was here."

I look at Tiff. "Why did you lie to me?"

She said, "Because I don't want you to be more stressed out while you are out there."

Karley says, "Daddy."

I say, "Yes, sweetheart?"

Karley asks, "Why did mommy and her doctor go into y'alls room?"

I look at Tiff. I carry Karley and put her to bed. I come out of Karley's room.

Tiff says, "I'm sorry for lying, but nothing happened with him. I swear, please forgive me."

I walk out. She follows, saying, "I will never lie to you again, I promise."

**

Mike said to the hostages, "It's okay, everything is okay."

They all clamored, saying, "Thank you."

Mike said, "Okay, okay. We have to be quiet as we get you outta here."

Mike and Tommy led the hostages up and out of the ship as crisp night air hit them. As they got to the docks, Mike and Tommy pointed the way for them to go. The hostages up and out of the ship as crisp night air hit them. As they got to the docks, Mike and Tommy pointed the way for them to go. The hostages ran to the police as Mike and Tommy slipped back into the shadows and came back to the car.

Mike said, "Hey, Lighthouse, did we get them all?"

Light replied, "Yes, you did. Good work!"

Mike said, "Thanks!"

Mike spent the rest of the night driving around and listening to the police scanner. When, at 10pm, it was apparent nothing was going on, Mike and Tommy went back in.

Mike made it back to the apartment shortly after 11:30pm. Linnea was still up watching TV. The Waveport news was just finishing a segment on the hostage rescue. Linnea ran up to Mike and passionately kissed him.

"You did good," Linnea said. "Let's go celebrate."

Mike and Linnea spent the night intertwined in romantic love making. They fell asleep in each other's arms.

As dawn broke, Mike awoke and made them breakfast in bed. Kissing Linnea, Mike said, "I have to go train. I love you."

Linnea replied, "I love you, too."

CHAPTER TEN

I go get my uniform and flew out and away. I went to my normal spot and sit on the ledge of the building. My phone rings. I don't answer. I put a dip in and spit and watch it hit the ground.

Hanna puts on her uniform and says, "I will be back. I'm going to look for Captain."

She leaves.

**

I hear, "Hey Cap, you ok?"

I ask, "What are you doing here?"

**

Tiff messages Linnea and tells her what happened and asks if Linnea can come over.

**

Hanna looks at me and says, "I'm here to bring you home." I hear Hanna say, "Ok, Bird Watch, I will."

She looks and says, "Captain, the Orator is the world leader and runs everything."

I said, "Great, that's just what we needed," as I hear, "Yes, it is."

As I see Billy, I shoot an arrow at him. It goes through him and he melts. Katie runs towards Hanna. As Katie swings, I jump on front of Hanna. As we fall over the ledge and start falling, I wrap my arms around her. I open my wings with one broken, I used the other to twist us as I hit the ground. We get up and they're gone. I look at Hanna and see blood.

I ask, "Are you ok?" as I feel the pain I my wings, arm, leg and back.

I pull her hood back. I see a cut on her cheek. She looks at me as I clean it up. She smiles and says, "You saved me."

I say, "Yes, I can't have you die."

She smiles. "Let's go home."

I hear her say, "Emerald to Bird Watch. Captain Arrow is hurt. We're coming in. Have Lt. Bass on standby."

"Bird Watch copies, Emerald Arrow."

**

Sammy comes in to sit with the kids as Tiff, Holly and Linnea run to the med bay.

**

As I teleported us into the command center. Hanna explained everything to Holly. As Tiff ran to me, my broken bones healed.

**

Mike and Linnea didn't want to part ways, but duty was calling. With another passionate kiss, Mike strode out the door. Mike went to the gym and found Tommy there.

"You must have had a good night!" Tommy greeted Mike with a smile.

Smiling back, Mike said, "Yes, yes I did. Ready for light training and more work?"

Tommy said, "Always ready."

Mike and Tommy warmed up and trained for two hours. That's when news about the injuries to Chris came in. Doctor

Cook was the one to deliver it.

Mike told Dr. Cook, "Damn, that is crazy. That could have been me."

Cook said, "Agreed. Reminds us to be extra careful."

Mike said, "We need basic first aid and field medicine training, just in case."

An idea came to Mike. Mike asked, "Will the whole healing thing work on me? That is twice that he's done the whole Lazarus or miracle healing act."

Doctor Cook said, "I'm not sure. I don't want to test it and find out either."

So, Mike and Tommy decided to take a few days off for training. The days were spent in lecture and labs. Mike spent the evenings with Linnea watching TV and making love. Life seemed perfect, to a point. That was until…
**

Hanna smiles and says, "That was amazing! Are you ok?"

I say, "Yes, are you?"

She says, "Yes."

Tiff hugs me and says, "I'm so sorry."

I get up and go to my office. I sit down. I put a dip in and relax.
**

Tiff tells Linnea, "I can feel he's still upset and hurt."

Hanna looks at Tiffinie and says, "It takes more than knowing how he feels."

"Also, it takes more than knowing you didn't sleep with the guy. It's all about trust, love, being there, and tell him everything."

Holly and Tiff look at each other.
**

Arial says, "Shut everything down and complete lockdown. No way in," as she hits the silent alarm.
**

I run to the command center. As I get there, so does everyone else. I get my uniform on and gear.

Arial says, "We have the World Military coming."

We have all of the villains coming with them. Holly laughs at me.

"They don't know about the underground base."

Arial says, "I have the entire base locked down, but they are headed this way. I can keep them out of the building, but we have to stay silent down here."

I tell Tiff, "Take the kids down into the silent room."

Tiff stops and says, "I love you, I'm truly sorry."

I look at her and say, "Go!" Our kids need to be safe, go now!"

She says, "But I have Linnea, Sammy and Chloe."

"Take her and all of the kids."

I have my soldiers stand guard all of the sealed entrances. I tell everyone to be ready as I hear through the comms Arial set up.

I hear them say, "We can't get in. The code isn't what it used to be. Well, the World Leader wants to use this base to stop the vigilantes by using us. Ok we will try again."

Arial laughs. "They can't beat me! Ha!"

**

Mike was sitting in class when the alarm went off. Mike told Doctor Cook that he had to go. Mike got up and rushed to the command center.

**

I stand behind Arial as I watch the enemy at the front door. Their guy starts cussing. Arial puts her hand over her mouth as she giggles. I smile.

Then, he says, "Let's try this another way, we have to get in."

Hanna comes up behind me. She puts a hand on my shoulder and asks, "What's going on?"

I say, "The same thing. They still ain't got in. Hopefully they don't."

Tiff comes up and asks if we can talk.

I ask, "Who has the kids?"

She says, "Lt. Bass does."

I say, "Let's go to my office."

We walk in silence. I shut the door. I ask, "What? We don't have time for this."

Tiff starts to cry. I take her into my arms and say, "I love you," as I kiss her. I use my thumb to wipe the tears off of her face and say, "Listen to me, go protect our kids."
**

Kevin comes up to Lt. Bass and asks, "Is everything ok?"

Holly says, "You mean to ask: is Captain Stamper around?"

Lt. Bass looks at him and asks, "What were you thinking. Dr. Blane. Captain Stamper will kill you if he sees you. So, you better get out of here before he comes down to check on his kids. Why did you come down here doctor, knowing the Captain's wife is supposed to be down here?"

He says, "I just wanted to check to see if everyone is ok. I also know what the Captain is thinking."

Lt. Bass says, "Duh, doctor!"

He says, "I know, but nothing happened."

Lt. Bass looks at him. "You are stupid, he knows how she feels at all times, they are connected, you can't lie to him."

Kevin says, "I know, but I can't help how she feels around me."
**

I look at Tiff and say, "I know how you feel about him and you lied."

Tiff looks at me and says, "Yes, I like him, but nothing happened. I'm in love with you and you're all I want. I promise to never to lie again to you."

As I hear Arial say, "Captain, get to the command center now."

I tell Tiffinie to get back to the sound proof safety room as we both run out.

I come into the command center. Arial says, "Captain, they are trying to torch the door.

I say, "Mike, Jacob, John, on me. We're going to teleport far enough out so they don't know we are in this base and we are going to stop them. No power, transmissions and communication to command center." I tell Jacob, "Use your strength, and also, use web. Tangle them up."

I tell Jacob, "Flank to the right." I look at Mike and say, "You flank to the left. Do what you have to." I tell John, "Cover our six, I'm taking them up the middle to draw them out. Then y'all come in behind them and we will fight in the tactical advantage here, they won't expect it. So, let's move out," as we got in our uniforms.

We teleport out and everyone goes to their positions.

I call out to the World Military. I yell, "Hey, stupid, this is a part of my city."

I hear, "Captain Stamper, stand down and surrender. You can't beat us all."

**

Jr asks mom, "Let me go help dad."
Tiff says, "No, your dad knows what he's doing."
**

As I hear "Get him," as they run towards me with guns drawn. They were all trained on me as I see Blue Hurricane take the guy out with the torch.

They start shooting at me. I stop all the guns and jam them as the bullets fell in front of me. I see Red Web and Blue Hurricane running towards us. I run and hit the first guy in formation. As we all fight, I kick one in the head and break another's neck. The villains run. I shoot arrows and killed more as I hear others yell retreat. I see a woman running. I shot four arrows, two in each ankle and two in each shoulder and pinned her to a tree.

**

Blue Hurricane was shooting air blasts left and right, pinning people and knocking soldiers off their feet. Soldiers seems to be filling in as soon as they were knocked out or killed. The press and impetus of the bodies was claustrophobic. Watching Captain Stamper's back was a full-time job.

The soldiers were trying to shoot at us. It was folly. Their bullets were stopped mid-air, falling uselessly to the ground.

Meanwhile, Mike walked with a purpose through the crowd. Slowly, anxiety crept into the soldier's eyes as they realized how futile their guns were. Mike continued to throw controlled gusts of air left and right, hitting soldier after soldier.

Anger crept into the back of Mike's mind as he took them down. Being Blue Hurricane worked out Mike's grief and frustration.

He shouted, "No! More! Death!" at the top of his lungs. Mike continued to manipulate the air.

Soon and finally, the soldiers began to thin out and fall away. Some panicked, dropping their guns and running. Others went berserk with fear, turning their guns to fully automatic fire and spraying and area. Bullets flew wildly, just as likely to hit a fellow soldier at this point has to be stopped by the hero's telekinesis and Blue Hurricane's wind abilities. The tide of the battle seemed to turn.

CHAPTER ELEVEN

I walk towards the woman I pinned. I hear, "Captain, no!" As I pull an arrow, I hear a gun shot. I continued walking as I hear another shot, then another. I drop to my knees as my vision gets blurry. I go to get up then another shot. I fall. My vision goes black.

**

Lt. Bass and Hanna comes in the command center. Arial looks at Holly and says, "He's going to kill her! They all retreated, we have to stop Captain."

Lt. Bass orders a sniper with tranquilizers to shoot and stop Captain Arrow. Holly yells, "Captain, no!" as Hanna started running towards Captain Arrow. Hanna jumps as she heard the shots while running as Hanna sees Captain Arrow fall.

Hanna gets to Chris. Hanna sits on the ground and takes my head and lays it in her lap. As she whispers it's ok, she runs her fingers through my hair. She holds me until they come out. Holly looks at Hanna.

"Let's get him in."

Soldiers take the woman and place her in a glass cell.
**

I wake up in bed. I see Tiff, Holly and Hanna.
I ask, "How long have I been out?"
Hanna says, "A couple of hours."
I get up and leave. Tiff says, "He's mad."
I go to my office. I get a dip. I sit and spit in an old Coke bottle. I hear a knock.
I ask, "Who is it?"
She says, "It's Holly."
I say, "Go away."
Holly begs, "Please, Chris, let me explain."
I spit, then say, "No. Lt. Bass."
She comes in. I say, "You had your commanding officers tranq'd in battle in front of my company."
Holly took my hand and said, "Chris, you had that same look in your eyes as you did the night your unit was ambushed."
I look at Holly and say, "She's part of the enemy who did it"
Holly interrupts, "But that girl doesn't deserve to die."
**

Blue Hurricane watched as Captain Stamper walked towards the pinned woman. Suddenly, a different sound cracked through the night as rifle shots rang out and darts flew through the air. Within a second or two, the tranquilizer fell Captain Stamper.

With renewed fury, Mike sent gust after gust at the enemy as some of them renewed their resolve. Yelling unintelligibly at the top of his lungs, Blue Hurricane cut through rank after rank. Soon, the soldiers had all fallen. Soon, the numbers of enemy soldiers finally dwindled to nothing. The battlefield was strewn with dead, wounded and unconscious.

Blue Hurricane contacted Lighthouse, saying, "The field is clear. These wounded needs medical help. We need to clear the area and repair it."

Lighthouse responded back, "You got it."

Crews worked through the night to clean up the mess left behind. As dawn broke, other than a few blood stains here and there, the outside looked like nothing happened.

Mike, leaving the battlefield, went back in, dressed down to civilian clothes, and went to find Linnea. Upon reaching the room, he embraced her and held her.

She whispered, "It's ok."

**

I look at her. I say, "She chose to be with them and she's a soldier."

I pull my hand away from Holly's. I stand and say, "She would have killed you if she had a chance."

Holly says, "We are heroes, Chris. We save people and you promised me you would try to stop killing. Here is your chance."

I say, "In a battle situation, you don't make that decision. I do."

Holly says, "I know that, Chris, but I care about you and I know that look in your eyes. Also, you would regret killing that girl. I know you."

I look at her and say, "I have done a lot I regret to protect the ones I love."

Holly says, "I know. Protect us in a different way."

Holly gets up with tears in her eyes and leaves.

I sit there until Tiff comes in with Jr and Karley. Tiff says, "I know how you are feeling and how you felt out there. I'm sorry."

Then Jr asks dad, "When can I start being a hero?"

I tell him, "After you finish school and grow up and learn how to be a hero."

Tiff says, "Take it easy on Holly, please. She only cares."

I say, "Yes, everyone cares too much to disobey me or lie, or cheat."

Her eyes get wide. She says, "I didn't do anything."

I say, "You have feelings for him, same thing."

She looks at me. "Please, Chris, stop! I'm in love with you."

They leave. I write a letter and leave it on my desk with my phone. The letter says, "I'm gone and since y'all can do this without me then do it good luck."

I teleport to the Bermuda Islands and walk into the triangle.
**

Tiff looks at Jr and says, "Something is wrong. I feel alone and disconnected."
**

Mike awoke the next day, sore from the previous day's fighting. A gentle fatigue had set in and his temples throbbed. Peace filled the bedroom as he lay with his arms wrapped around Linnea. Slowly, Mike extracted his arms and got up. Linnea groaned slightly as he did so.

"Life is good," Mike thought, as he went to the kitchen for an energy drink. Sipping it deeply, Mike let the carbonation fill his mouth and stomach. "Time for breakfast," he said, to no one in particular.

Cooking up eggs, bacon and potatoes (hash brown style), Mike made two plates. Bringing them into the bedroom, Linnea and Mike enjoyed the peace.
**

Travis stared agape at the battlefield below. This should have been an easy go-in-and-occupy job. The Orator would be angry. Travis watched as the inadequate soldiers attacked Captain Stamper and his motley crew. Nothing was working.

As the short battle raged on, he watched as most of his soldiers were knocked out or killed. Travis blended in with the scenery, leaving in disgust. Travis' rage boiled as he left. Where, in god's name, had they come from? It was like they knew what was going on.

"We have a mole," Travis thought bitterly, sure of it being the only excuse.
**

Tiff messages everyone to check on them. Everyone messages

back except Chris. Holly and Hanna went to Chris' office. They knock and there's no answer. Holly opens the door and sees the letter and phone on the desk. Lt. Bass calls all the heroes to the command center.

Lt. Bass briefed everyone on the situation, then she looks at Tiff.

Holly asks, "Where could he be able to lose complete connection with you?"

Tiff says, "Has to be the Bermuda Triangle."

Lt. Bass says, "Hanna, go find the Captain and get him back." Lt. Bass says, "I will watch over Raven City until you get back with him."

**

I sit and watch the waves roll in as I smile, siting at the edge of the cave.

**

Hanna asks Tiff to teleport her there. So, she does, then teleports back. Hanna takes a deep breath and steps into the unknown. As she gets confused while walking through the heavy, dense forest on the island. Hanna stumbles through a brush as she steps then hears the trap go off. Hanna closes her eyes as she hears the snap, she feels something around her waist.

Hanna screams as she gets hit by something then lands on it. She waits for the pain then opens her eyes and sees she landed on me.

**

I look at Hanna and ask, "What are you doing here?"

Hanna says, "To bring you home."

I say, "No, y'all don't need me."

Hanna looks at me and says, "Chris, I need you. So does everyone else. Also, why do I feel strange?"

I look at her. I say, "It's got to be the Bermuda Triangle. Let's rest, I need a break."

She says, "Ok, but let's head back tomorrow."

**

"So, Chris is gone," Mike thinks, as he spars with Tommy.

The city was quiet tonight as they practiced in uniform. Nothing could break the calm Mike still felt. It felt great thrashing some bad guys. Maybe too great.

The rest of the night was quiet, with everyone staying indoors just in case.

**

Orator says, "Bring them in here, now!" as Travis, Billy and Lin Chi come in. "How could this happen?" he yelled. "I want them found and dead. No mistakes this time. Always be on guard. I better not see any of y'all until they are all dead or you will die also."

They leave. Billy says, "I'm already dead." Everyone laughs.

"Well, who knows how to find and fight them one at a time?"

Bessie says, "Attack the cities one at a time. Let's all get to work and let's kill them."

President Wayne says, "Let's pardon all crimes against the vigilantes so they will come out and put vigilante task force in those cities. So, they do come out, let them try to have a normal life. We can't let the world know these people even exist."

Katie says, "Dad, everyone knows there are people with abilities in those four cities."

Wayne says, "I don't care! Let's put an end to them. Let's send all of you guys into all four cities. Let's tear the cities down."

Katie says, "I want Raven City."

Wayne says, "If you take Lin Chi with you."

"Alright, dad, I will."

Katie looks at Lin Chi and says, "Stay out of my way."

They left as the two women stand on the building where they attacked Chris and a girl he called Emerald. Katie points at a police vehicle that pulls up at a convenience store as they watch her go in. As the Detective walks out, Katie says, "Hey Detective?"

Juliet asks, "Yes?"
Katie asks, as she pulls out a picture, "Do you know him?"
Juliet says, "Yes."
Then Lin Chi comes up behind Juliet and knocks her out.

CHAPTER TWELVE

I feel someone touch me. I wake up. I see Hanna cuddled up next to me. I ask her if she's ok.

She says, "I don't feel good and I'm cold."

I sit her up and pull her hood down to see fer face. She was extremely pale. I touch her forehead. She was burning up.

I look at her and say, "Hanna, you're sick. I need to get you back to the base now."

I pick her up and she wraps her arms around my neck as her head drops on my shoulder. I teleport back to base and walk into med bay with Hanna in my arms. Holly was sitting there when I walked in. I told Holly Hanna's symptoms.

Holly said, "Please, Captain, go to the waiting room," as more nurses and doctors came in.

My phone rings. I see a text from Juliet saying we have the beautiful Detective Nielson.

As Lt. Bass comes out from the back, she sees that look on my face.

Holly says, "Go. I got Hanna," as the alarm sounded.

Arial says, "Hey boss," as I come in.

Arial pulls up the news as everyone comes into the command center. As a video of Detective Nielson and a voice says, "Captain Arrow, you have a choice to make. Pick between Detective Nielson's life or all four cities' complete destruction. All four cities are rigged to blow along with this building Detective Nielson is in. So, pick."

As the World Military shows up to back them up. I look at everyone and say, "We will have to kill without hesitation to save everyone."

I tell everyone to find the explosives in your cities. "When you do, let me know. Disconnect those explosives at the same time. Go now!"

As I run to fly out, Tabitha says, "Please let me help." So, I let her out. She morphs and we fly out.

**

Mike awoke the next day refreshed and thirsty. Thirsty for the next round of action. It was a bad omen for them the news came in about the bombs. At least, Chris was back to making decisions. That made Mike feel more comfortable. Mike went to find Tommy.

"Suit up, Tommy," Mike said. "Big things are happening."

"I heard," Tommy replied.

By this time, everyone in the complex had heard. They went to go suit up. They then went to the vehicle bays and started up the SUV.

"What's the word, Lighthouse? What are we doing?" Mike said.

"You need to be directed to the bomb, disarm it at the same time as the other ones, and then celebrate a victory," Lighthouse replied.

Mike said, "Something tells me it won't be that easy. The bombs are going to be guarded, aren't they?"

"Yeah, something like that," Lighthouse almost whispered.

Mike took a deep breath, mentally becoming Blue Hurricane.

Blue Hurricane smiled to himself as he shifted the vehicle into drive. Blue Hurricane drove towards Wave City at just above the speed limit, not wanting to attract attention from police. After all, they were just doing their jobs.

Upon reaching Wave City, he began to take directions from Lighthouse. Blue Hurricane took a left here and a right there, inching towards the destination.

**

We land as we see people running and panicking everywhere. I climb on top of a car and yell as the news station pointed their cameras at me.

I say, "Everyone calm down. This is my city. We will stand and protect our city."

I see three units of the World Military coming as I told everyone to evacuate now. Everyone runs. I look around. Tabitha is gone as I hear, "Freeze, Captain Arrow! You're under arrest."

I say, "Of course," as they close in on me. I jump off the car. I use telekinesis to throw as many as I can. A taser hits me I hit my knees then I see the guy that tased me hit the ground. I get up and start shooting arrows and Tabitha smiles and says, "I'm not leaving your side."

I tell her, "Go get everyone out of that part of the city. I am going after the Detective."

She takes off as I kill a few more then teleport to the location. As I enter the building, I get hit. I see Katie. She smiles.

"I hope your partner can save herself. It's Emerald Arrow, right?"

I say, "No," and hit Katie. Tabitha sees Lin Chi, and Lin Chi smiles.

"Let's end this city."

Tabitha morphs and hits Lin Chi into a wall as they fight.

Katie gets up and swings at me as I grab her and flip her, then I shoot an arrow through her knee. She laughs and pulls it out and stabs me. She asks, "Are you like me," as I shoot another arrow through her chest. Then I break her neck. I lay her gently on the ground as I teleport into the room where I see Juliet tied up in a chair. I look at her. She looks like she's been beaten. I tell her, "Don't move." She looks at me then looks down.

**

As Blue Hurricane rounds the final corner, he finds himself on a four block straight away street that dead ends at the Wave City Courthouse. Even at this distance, Blue Hurricane could see several units of the World Military on alert outside.

The city blocks were lined on either side with historical stone and brick buildings. Inside, the aged buildings were tiny mom-and-pop shops that were the bulk of the downtown economy. At the end of this stood a stark contrast of fatigues and metal. The World Military had brought a tank this time.

The tank's menacing barrel gleamed in the street lamps hazed glow. Blue Hurricane stopped the SUV and got out.

**

Tommy Hale, a.k.a. Waterspout, stood behind Blue Hurricane. Unsure of his ability to help, a shiver raced down his spine. He had to trust his leader's ability to help the city and protect him. Waterspout checked his pistol and grabbed his rifle. Soon, all hell would be unleashed in downtown Wave Port City.

**

Blue Hurricane watched the World Military as Tommy fidgeted. Both sides seemed on edge. Mike didn't know what to do other than fly straight down the middle. Blue Hurricane had to succeed. Blue Hurricane had to win. He began to summon his power to shield Waterspout and himself. It was time.

**

Juliet asks, "Why didn't you tell me?"

I ask her, "What do you mean?"

Juliet said, "I'm not stupid, Chris. They kidnapped me to get to you. They showed me a picture of you."

I pulled my hood back. I looked into her eyes as I cleaned her wounds. I say, "I'm sorry, I shouldn't have talked to you and put you in danger."

She smiles. "You're stupid. I'm a cop and I talked to you first."

I say, "So, I didn't have to continue."

She interrupts. "Shut up, Chris. Also, no, I'm not going to arrest you, Chris, because I like you."

I ask, "What is it with you women? I'm married."

She laughs. "Because you're funny and a good man."

I get light-headed. I look down. I see a lot of blood. I feel the pain. I stop the bleeding. I tell her to sit still until I get the call to start. I speak into my earpiece. "When you find the bombs, disarm them at the same time to save the other three cities. Tabitha, find the one in Raven and do the same."

They all say, "10-4, we copy."

We sit there waiting as Tabitha looks at Lin Chi and says sorry, I got to hurry.

Tabitha pulls out a tranq arrow and stabbed Lin Chi with it as Lin Chi fell over. Tabitha tied her up and took off to find the bomb. Time passes. I say report in. Voices came back. "Sorry, Captain, but we're tied up fighting," as Red Web says, "Captain, we found it and standing by."

I say, "I found the Detective."

Captain Cross comes through, "We have enhanced villains."

I said, "Yes, they are metahuman. Take them out."

Captain Cross, "We have to get the bombs. Ok Captain Arrow."

Juliet says, "You know all of the heroes." I smile. "And you all work together."

I say, "Yes."

**

The first shot came from the tank with a resounding noise. Blue Hurricane flew with Waterspout towards it. Blue Hurricane deflected the round at the last second. Flying closer and closer, small arms fire hit the shield and fell to the ground.

Waterspout opened up with his rifle, firing almost blindly at the combatants. Still, he was taking them out. That was when Blue Hurricane summoned a tornado into the crowd. Debris, people and weapons flew round and round. Scores of combatants tried to hunker down, but to no avail. The tank fought to stay right side up.

In a flash, in an instant, the World Military units were decimated. Blue Hurricane flew on to the courthouse. Entering into the limestone building was like night and day. It was peaceful and serene. Here was where the bomb was located.

Blue Hurricane spoke into the headset. "Lighthouse, inside the courthouse. We're searching for the bomb."

"Roger that," Lighthouse replied.

Blue Hurricane and Tommy split up and began frantically searching, room by room they went. Dread began to creep into Mike's head as he started doubting if the bomb existed. Finally, Mike found it in a second-floor judge's chambers.

"Lighthouse, we found it," Blue Hurricane radioed.

CHAPTER THIRTEEN

I hear Blue Hurricane say, "Lighthouse, we found it."
I say, "Bird Watch."
She says, "Go ahead, Captain."
I say, "Connect us all together."
She says, "Copy that, Captain."
I say, "Everyone report in."
Blue Hurricane says, "Captain Arrow, we found our bomb."
Captain Cross says, "We found ours."
Red Web says, "We found ours."
Tabitha says, "Found ours, Captain."
I say, "Everyone get your partners out first. They're human."
Everyone says, "Done."
I ask, "Do you see the green and red wires?"
They say, "Yes."
I said, "Y'all cut both all on the count of three."
They said, "We copy, Captain," as Tabitha asks, "How will you disable the one that pressured by the Detective?"
I say, "I can't without blowing up the other four bombs."

I say, "One."

Then I hear, "Bird Watch to Captain Arrow."

Lt. Bass says, "Emerald Arrow is gone."

I say, "Find her, she couldn't have left by herself. Two."

I move to Juliet and put my arms around her as I hug her. As I say "three," everyone cuts their wires. I hear the explosion and I feel the heat as I try to protect Juliet.

**

Tabitha cuts the wire. She hears a big explosion to the south side of Raven City. She sees a big cloud of smoke and fire as she sees first responders racing to get there.

Tabitha asks, "Captain, are you ok?"

All she hears is static as Bird Watch says, "We lost all connection with Captain. But all four cities are safe except the south side of Raven City."

Bird Watch tells Tabitha to "go and find our Captain. I'm sure he's safe."

So, Tabitha took off to help search and rescue the victims of the bomb.

**

Blue Hurricane closes his eyes as he cut the wired. An audible snick and that was it. Mike blinked and looked around. That was when Blue Hurricane heard over the radio, "We lost connection with the Captain."

Blue Hurricane muttered to himself, "Missing again? Really?"

Leaving the courthouse, Blue Hurricane radioed to Waterspout, "Waterspout, come pick me up. We're going to Raven City to help clean up and search for survivors. It's going to be a long night."

"Will comply," Waterspout said.

A minute later, the SUV pulled up right next to Blue Hurricane.

Tommy drove on the way saying, "Did you hear about the Captain?"

"Yeah, I did. He probably teleported to safety or Bermuda or something."

The rest of the ride was spent in silence.

Upon reaching the scene, the area looked like a warzone. Rubble and debris were everywhere. Ambulances and police vehicles formed a blockade. Upon reaching the barricade, a young officer was on watch.

"Hey, it's you. Have you come to help?"

"Yes," Blue Hurricane replied.

The officer rushed them in. They spent the night saving people trapped in the debris and clearing up the mess.

**

As all four of the Mayors stand to make a press conference, Mayor Nielson starts by saying, "I give my deepest condolences to the victims' families of the bombing in the south side of Raven City. There are thousands confirmed dead and MIA." Tears roll down her face as she says, "The vigilantes chose to save the cities. They saved millions. They took the least number of casualties and my sister could be one."

**

I hear Juliet say, "Chris, you can let me go," as she's laying on top of me.

I unwrap my wings and arms from around her. I hear a giggle. I look up to see Hanna and Tabitha. I get up and hug her. She smiles. I touch Hanna's head and say, "You're burning up." She smiles and opens her wings and opens her hand as it flames up.

Hanna says, "I'm like you," as I open my hand and it flames up.

Juliet says, "You will have to explain it all one day."

I tell Tabitha and Hanna to head back and they leave. I change my clothes. As Juliet and I walk out of the rubble, Juliet saw blood running from my head and said, "You're covered in dirt."

I laugh, and say, "Yes, I am. I just saved you from a bomb. So are you."

Juliet sees the camera crews and her sister. Juliet grabs my hand and pulls me, saying, "Come on!"

I say, "Detective?"

She turns and says, "Don't worry."

As Juliet pulls me behind her as a woman screams and runs and hugs her. As Mayor Nielson turned and saw Molly hugging Juliet as she runs to her sisters. Amy and Molly look at me.

Amy asks Juliet, "Who is he?"

Juliet says, "His name is Chris. He saved me from the bomb."

Amy and Molly hug me and says, "Thank you," as Amy pulled me to her side as the reporters started asking questions. As voices rang out saying, "Captain Chris Stamper, you're under arrest."

**

Blue Hurricane gingerly lifted block after block of debris using his abilities. Exposing some survivors, but many deceased. Saying a silent prayer for each person revealed. A couple of hours passes. Soon, voices and a ruckus filled the air behind Blue Hurricane and Waterspout. Next thing they knew, the young officer was dragging them to a hiding spot.

"Listen, y'all better leave here. The World Military wants to arrest you," the officer told them.

"Alright, thank you, Officer Nelson. Stay safe and don't get in trouble because of us," Blue Hurricane replied.

Quickly and quietly, Blue Hurricane and Waterspout rushed back to the SUV.

Driving back to the hideout, they avoided all detection due to the commotion at the bomb site. Parking the car, Tommy said, "Phew, that was close. Glad we didn't have to fight again."

"Agreed. They are just following orders, but damn. Last thing we need is another fight." Blue Hurricane sighed as he agreed.

"Blue Hurricane to Lighthouse. We're back home after being chased by the World Military. We are calling it a night," Mike said into the radio.

"Copy that. Good work tonight," Lighthouse responded.

"Thanks," Mike said.

Mike went back to the apartment, stripped down and took a

much-deserved shower.

**

Mayor Nielson looks at me and says, "Captain Stamper?" as the World Military comes up and puts me in handcuffs.

Mayor Nielson says, "I'm pardoning Captain Stamper of any and all crimes, for saving several lives and Detective Nielson's life."

The World Military says, "Sorry, that's not going to work."

Mayor Nielson said, "The world government dropped all charges against Captain Stamper and Universe Labs."

They look at her as the other three Mayors step up with city law enforcement. Juliet hugs me then says, "He's not going anywhere," as the World Military commander says, "Ok. It's true Orator said that. Let's go."

Amy hugs me and says, "Thank you for saving my sister. I'm glad you found her."

I get ready to leave. She says, "Stay, you need looked at plus you're safe from the world government now."

As the reporters crowd us, I whisper to Juliet and say, "I have to end this now!"

She whispers, "Be careful."

I say, "It's ok," as Amy announces to the press that she is running for governor. Amy whispers to Juliet as Amy pulls me to her.

"Mr. Stamper is running for Mayor," Amy says. "I give him my full support and I am backing his campaign."

I say, "Thank you, Mayor Nielson. I will do my best," and she smiles and says, "I will help you."

As I get away and make it back to the command center, I sit down I can hear the news repeating the day's events. Tiff hugs and kisses me and says, "I'm proud of you."

I say, "Let's go to Mike's and Linnea's apartment."

As the women talk, me and Mike discussed what happened.

I ask, "If I win as Mayor, do you want a job in my administration

so we can live a somewhat normal life? We will stop the world government and stop the Orator."
**

Mike thoughtfully considered what was being proposed. Sighing loudly, he shook his head.

"What you're suggesting has appeal. And what we are doing right now has impact on lives. Can we really escape doing the costumed hero thing? If so, should we? Can I do both?"

Mike let his words hang in the air.

"If so, then we should. If not, let's see where normal gets us."
**

I look at Mike and say, "We can do both. No one knows it's us and this gives us an advantage. We get more use of law enforcement. We get the scoop on all crimes in all four cities. We get to react faster as far as normal goes. We're super heroes. Both has an impact on lives. We now can fight in the day and night. This gives us a normal job. Of course, we can use being the Mayor as cover."

I say, "We need to let the world government think we're in one place except here. Keep our wives and kids here safe until the world government is gone. Let's take this and stop the world government so we can live a normal life. Yes, we can come in to the base to see our wives and kids. This helps us get close to stopping Orator. When we get the shot, we can't miss."

"I know the Orator will have someone run against me, but we can win the election. You can come let me know when you decide. Goodnight." And I told Mike, "Good job today."

We left and we go back to our apartment.

Tiff asks, "What's wrong babe? I can feel what you do."

I said, "Well, Tiff, I feel alone everyone seems like they don't want me around, even you."

She looks shocked and says, "Chris, you know that's not true."

I say, "Well prove it."

I put a dip in and walk to the couch as Karley comes running into my arms. Karley screams, "Daddy!" I laugh as I pick her up.

Tiff says, "See, we all need you. There's your proof. I love you and want and need you, too."

I ask Karley, "What are you doing up, baby?"

She says, "Waiting on you, daddy, I want a bed time story and to be tucked in."

So, I pick her up and tuck her in and read her to sleep. I kiss her on the head then turn her nightlight on. I sit on the couch and me and Tiff talk as she starts to cry.

She says, "Please, Chris, I love you, not him."

I wipe the tears from her eyes. I say, "You make the decision what we do with him. I know every time I leave, Dr. Blane sneaks around to you."

She says, "Yes, he has."

I tell her, "Choose."

She gets mad. Tiff gets silent as I stand up and walk to the bedroom. I lay down and fall asleep. Tiff gets undressed and crawls into the bed and wakes me up and says, "You know I always choose you."

As we make love then go to sleep together.
**

Amy looks at Juliet and says, "Chris is 18. He was a Captain in the U.S. Army also assigned to Universe Labs. It shows. Oh wow, look Juliet," she says, "No, he will tell me when he's ready."
**

Dr. Blane is on the phone and says, "Yes sir, that will be easy. It will be ready for the swearing into office."
**

Tiff opens the door to see Lt. Bass and as Tiff lets her in Holly tells Tiff what she heard.

Tiff said, "I will let Chris know when he gets up."

Holly says, "Thanks, goodnight."

Tiff lets her out and goes back to bed. As she crawls back into bed, I ask, "What was that about?"

Tiff said, "It was about Dr. Blane, not important. It sounds like he's got a surprise for you if you win the election," as we both go to sleep.

**

Mike flops down on the couch next to Linnea. Sighing heavily, Mike says, "Well, I guess I'm going to help Chris out. What do you think?"

Linnea got really thoughtful for a second. She then replied, "If after it's done, we can have a normal life, then you need to do it."

Mike turned to her and said, "It's going to mean longer hours, but I think we need to just stay safe."

Mike leaned in and kissed Linnea. They kicked back and played video games for an hour or two in near silence, each thinking of the long road ahead of them and the road behind them. They knew that the hardest choices lay before them. Both Mike and Linnea also knew that they had each other, which was no small thing.

Mike and Linnea went to bed in each other's arms, not wanting to let each other go. Mike dreamt of a scene of destruction unfolding before him. Thousands of body parts lay in a mess of twisted concrete and metal. Mike shivered unconsciously at this thought. Linnea held him tighter as a result. Her own dreams turning to similar things.

Mike woke up, still groggy from a fitful sleep. He walked into the kitchen and popped a cold energy drink. Sipping it thoughtfully, Mike tried and failed to recall the dream he had. Mike wondered why it seemed so important. Mike spent the morning making breakfast and researching being part of the administration.

Chapter Fourteen

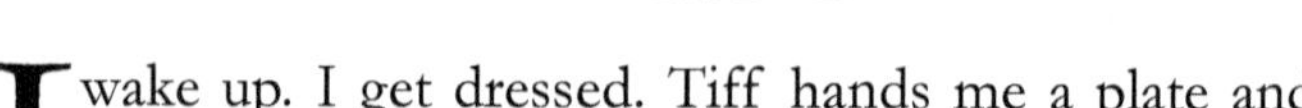

I wake up. I get dressed. Tiff hands me a plate and Jr asks, "Dad, can I go with you today?"

I say, "No, it's still too dangerous with the World Military out there.

Tiff hands me a can of dip and I kiss everyone goodbye. I go to my office. Hanna comes in and asks, "Can I be your secretary when you become Mayor?"

I smile. "Of course, but it starts now," as my phone rings I say, "Hello, this is Chris."

Juliet says, "Good morning. Me and Amy need to meet up with you asap. You need to be in a suit or tux and give me an address to pick you up."

Hanna hands me a suit and I say I will be waiting at the corner of Terrel and Mark be there in an hour. So, I tell Hanna to take all my calls. She smiles. "Yes, sir." I wait. I see a limousine pull up. The driver gets out and opens the door.

Amy and Juliet say, "Get in." I see the Mayor symbol on the car as the driver says "sir" as I get in.

Amy says, "You have a press conference and so far, no one opposes you."

I said, "That's shocking," as the door is opened and I get out as I help the women out of the car. As they wrap an arm around each of my arms, I escort them in as cameras flash. They smile. I say you both look beautiful as the cops escort us through.

We come to the stage as Amy says, "Chris Stamper is running unopposed. So, in two weeks. Mr. Stamper will win and be sworn in."

There was clapping as my campaign manager sits behind me. Amy introduced me. The questions started. I answered them.

One asked, "What is your plan for south side?"

I say, "Rebuild and honor the fallen."

"The people hold the vigilantes accountable for the bombing and they want justice, what are you going to do?"

I say, "I'm going to make the people who hurt my city pay for this!"

They clap. Amy says, "Enough," as the campaign manager and both women guide me off of the stage.

**

Bessie says, "I like that idea, but we're down three people."

Wayne laughs. "We have one extra. Don't forget, we have all the low lives of the world and assassins."

She laughs. "You're right. I will go looking for them."

He says, "No, everything is lined up. No work for you."

Orator says, "We want him to win. He won't survive being sworn in. I know he will not live or anyone there."

**

As we sit down to eat, Amy and Juliet smiles at me and say, "You did amazing up there today."

I say, "Thank y'all."

Amy says, "Chris, in two weeks all of the state elections will be final."

I look at her. "We will win, no problem.

As the local news came on saying, "The Mayor candidate, Chris Stamper, made a strong statement today. He had governor candidate Amy Nielson and Detective Juliet Nielson on both arms.

Who is this guy? He was a nobody, Bob, have you ever heard of this guy?"

He says, "Only once, Chelsy."

"Well, we will see, he seems level-headed and he will get justice for our city," as my phone rings I look.

Amy says, "Answer it."

I do. I say, "Go ahead."

Karley asks, "Daddy, when are you coming home? I want to spend the day with you."

I say, "Well, sweetheart, daddy has to finish up with work."

Amy and Juliet look at each other. I tell Karley, "I will be home soon. I love you too," as I hang up.

They look at me and ask, "You have kids?"

I say, "A son and a daughter."

Juliet looks down. "I'm sorry, Chris."

I ask, "What?"

Juliet says, "I should have asked if you had kids or even single."

Amy says, "This needs to stay between us."

Juliet says, "Sorry to assume anything."

I ask, "What do you mean? I keep that part of my life away because the issues I have with her mom."

Juliet looks at me with hope in her eyes as I get up, pay the bill, and leave.

Amy says, "So, he had kids, we can spin all of it our way if it's ever needed."

Juliet says, "I'm not giving up," as she thinks "he saved me when he didn't have to. He came for me himself just for me."

I take my time and walk as I look and see the news media coming up so I run as they speed up. I round a corner then I teleport back home.

**

Holly follows Dr. Kevin as Holly hides, watches, and videos it as Tiffinie shows up. Tiff kisses Kevin and asks, "Is the surprise ready for Chris?"

He says, "Yes, it's ready. Just after he is sworn in, he will be surprised."

As they kiss, he opens the door and they go in together. Holly waits. They come out forty minutes later. They were fixing their clothes.

She said, "That was fun."

They kiss and go their own way. Holly was shocked and says, "He has to know."

**

I sit down in my office. There's a knock on the door as I get a dip. I say come in as Holly came in looking pale. I ask, "What's wrong." She hands me her phone. I watch the video. I look at her and I send it to my phone. I hand her phone back to her and walk out.

I go to the command center and put my uniform on and hear Holly say, "Chris, they're not worth it."

Hanna comes in and see what's going on. Hanna sees the look in my eyes as Holly did and Hanna says, "I don't know what's going on, but Chris, don't"

As Tiff comes in and asks, "What's going on?"

Then Dr. Blane comes in. I teleport right in front of Dr. Blane and grab him by his throat.

I slam him against the wall as all three women come running as I hit him. As he asks through the blood pouring from his face, "What did I do this time?"

"I told you to stay away from Tiff. Like I told her to stay away from you."

Tiff says, "We have done what you said, we haven't."

I say, "Oh yeah?"

He says, "Yes, it's true."

I pull my phone out and played the video for him to see as his eyes got wide. I show it to Tiff. She couldn't look at me. I hit him again and say, "Both of you are liars."

Holly calls the soldiers in as I throw him down as he slides down the wall.

**

Mike gets dressed after waking up late and calls Tommy. Tommy answers and says, "Hello, Mike, how can I help you?"

Mike said, "Want to go out tonight? And work the streets that is?"

Tommy replied, "Yes! I am going stir crazy!"

"Meet me at 5pm in uniform," Mike said.

They day ticked by slowly and steadily. Mike spent the day watching TV with Linnea. Both were anxious for what the night would provide. Both nervous for the safety of Mike. The hour quickly approached where it was time to go. At 3pm, Linnea and Mike made love as if it was their last time on earth. Then Mike took a long, hot shower. His mind slowly focusing on his night ahead.

Blue Hurricane met Waterspout at the designated spot and both walked to the SUV together. The silence built as they walked to the car. Both realizing how dangerous this could be with the World Military on their case. Both realizing how necessary this was for them.

Blue Hurricane put the ear piece in and keyed the microphone. "Blue Hurricane to Lighthouse, we're about to head out. Anything on the scanners?"

Lighthouse responded, "Nothing yet. Drive to Waveport City and we'll get you something, I am sure.

So Blue Hurricane ordered Tommy to go. Tommy threw the car into drive and pulled out.

**

Tiff says, "It's not what it looks like."

I say, "Quit lying! Get your stuff out of my apartment or

when I get home, I'm getting mine and leaving."

She begs, "Please, Chris, don't do this.

"Too late, you did this, not me."

She can feel my heart breaking as I walk away. I sit down in my office. It's silent. No one bothers me.

I sit there dipping. My phone rings. I say, "Chris." I hear Juliet say, "Hey Chris, you have another press conference tomorrow."

I say, "Ok, no problem. What time?"

"10 am."

I say, "Meet y'all there."

She says, "Ok."

I leave the office. I head home. I come into the apartment Tiff was sitting there. I walk past her. I go pack my stuff up as Karley meets me at the door. Karley asks, "Can I go with you, daddy?"

I say, "Yes."

Jr says, "I'm staying with mom."

I get Karley's stuff and we walk to a new apartment. We walk in. I took Karley to her new room and got her to bed. I sit on the couch and drink some whiskey. There's a knock on the door. I open the door. I see Mike and Linnea. I tell them to come in. They come in and sit on the couch.

Mike said, "I went to your apartment to tell you I accept the position on the administration."

Linnea says, "If it gets us back to a normal life."

I smile and say, "As normal as super humans can get."

Mike asks, "Why did you move out and away from Tiffinie?"

I showed him and Linnea the video. I tell Mike, "You're going to be Chief of Staff right under the major. Mike, we have a press conference at 10 am."

He says, "Ok, I will meet you there."

They said, "Goodnight," and left as there's another knock on the door. I see Hanna. She says, "I can't sleep." She takes the alcohol out of my hand and says, "You don't need this."

I fall asleep on the couch. She goes to sleep in my room.

**

Blue Hurricane and Waterspout made it to Waveport City without incident. During the drive, Blue Hurricane thought of the position he just accepted and the responsibility it entailed. They began to drive in a wide circle when Lighthouse said, "We've got a couple of looters near you, Hurricane. Want to take 'em?"

"Yes, give me the address," Blue Hurricane responded.

He plugged the address into the GPS and let it guide them. Ahead of them was the shopping district of Waveport. The particular shop being looted was a jewelry store named Abel's Fine Jewelry. Stopping a block from the place, Blue Hurricane and Waterspout flew in.

**

The looters lay in wait for the vigilantes to show up, confident having military backup would save them. One perked up.

"Here they come," he said into the mic, raising his machine gun. The others did likewise.

**

Flying in, Mike noticed no police. "Weird," he thought, and created a shield around him. That was when all hell broke loose. Bullets rained down and towards him. It was a trap! Waterspout fired at the rooftop overwatch, cleanly taking them out. Mike removed the air from the jewelry store, suffocating the remaining assailants. Once the firefight ended, Mike checked the bodies to find World Military uniforms underneath.

**

I wake up to the smell of cooking. I sit up. I hear a woman say, "Coffee is ready. So is Karley."

I go get changed into a suit and tie. Hanna says, "Come eat." She says, "By the way, you clean up nice."

I say, "Thanks. Can you take Karley and drop her off to Tiffinie?"

"Of course, I can do that for you. Here is your dip and good luck today."

I text Mike and say, "Let's get to Terrel Street and meet Amy and Juliet."

I leave to meet Mike. I kiss Karley on the head and leave.

**

Hanna picks Karley up as they make it to Tiff's apartment. She knocks. Tiffinie opens the door with her face red and swollen from crying. As Tiff lets Karley in, Tiff asked, "Did you stay with Chris last night?"

Hanna said, "Yes, Chris was drinking. I took care of Karley and, no, we didn't sleep together. He passed out on the couch. He's hurt, so, no, I won't take advantage of that."

Tiff says, "Sorry, you're a good friend to him."

Yes, I am, Tiffinie, and I won't hurt him. Neither will Holly."

Tiff says, "It really isn't what you guys think it is."

Hanna says, "I'm there to help him, not judge you. It's for y'all to work out."

As she leaves and cleans up the apartment.

**

I see Mike as the Mayor's limo pulls up the driver lets us in. I introduce Mike to Amy and Juliet. I tell them, "Mike is going to be Chief of Staff." Amy smiles.

"I hope you men can handle the press." She laughs.

Juliet says, "Nice to meet you, Mike. I'm a Detective and I have to work after this."

As the car stops, I escort Juliet. Amy asks Mike to escort her.

**

Mike says, "Of course. And how are you this fine morning, Amy?"

Amy answered, "Good, and you?"

"I'm great. So, what is your role here? I mean, in this campaign."

"I've been acting as an advisor. Having done this job before, I know how all this works. And what we need to know, is about you. We don't know hardly anything about you. What is your motivation here?" Amy asked.

Mike thought about his answer. He knew the answer had to reveal personality, but conceal the true motivation.

Mike sighed softly. "I've known Chris for a while. He went to my school. All we've wanted was a normal, easy life. We wanted to protect freedom and the right to choose a good way of life. I'm here to make sure Chris has all he needs to continue to support that. At the same time, the people need true justice for the heinous attack on our city, perpetrated by a villainous group," Mike continued.

Amy was misty eyed at Mike's altruism. "Wow," she said. "You sound committed to this cause."

Mike said, "More than words can ever describe. If me sacrificing my time can help make my wife's life even better. I am going to do it. I will do anything for her."

CHAPTER FIFTEEN

As we escort the women in, the reporters and newspapers take pictures of us all together. Amy takes the microphone and introduced me. As they clap, I introduce Mike Smith as Chief of Staff. They clap. They ask, "Mr. Smith, what's your plan to help this city?"

I go to step up. He smiles and gestures. "I got this, trust me," as he says, "Just like Chris has said, we will rebuild the south side of Raven City.

"Also, to get justice for all of the fallen of south side. We will prevail in all four of these cities." As they clap, so does Amy and Juliet. Mike says, "Here is Mr. Stamper, your soon-to-be Mayor."

They clap as I step up. I bring Juliet up and introduce her. I say, "We are working hand-in-hand with law enforcement to put a stop to and to put the ones responsible for this behind bars.

The World Military comes in and watches the press conference. I see the FBI with them. I say, "Let's go," as the four of us end the press conference and head towards the door.

I hear, "Captain Stamper, can we talk to you and Mr. Smith?"

Juliet and Amy states, "They're not going without us."

They say, "Ok, let's go," as we get in the Mayor's limousine.

Mike whispers, "Dang, they are here, too!"

I whisper very low, "What do you mean?"

Mike whispers, "Oh yeah, we can hear each other. Super hearing. Last night, Tommy and I went out to Waveport and got called out to some looters. It was a setup by the World Military."

As the limo had an escort by the FBI and World Military. We stop. I open the door, get out and I help the women out, then Mike stands next to me. I see Gen Willson and Commander Moris.

They say, "Good to see you, Captain."

Gen Willson asked, "Can we talk in private, Captain?"

Juliet, Mike and Amy say, "Not without us."

I say, "It's ok. Juliet, come with me," and I ask Mike to get Amy out of here if something happens so stay with Amy.

**

Mike shuffled back and forth as he began his wait anxiously. He recognized General Wilson from the beginning and hoped that would bode well for them. Amy could see the tension that was building in Mike's features and sought to ease it with small talk.

She asked, "Tell me about your wife. What is she like?"

Recognizing the strategy she was using, he sighed. Mike stopped shuffling and gave in.

"She is wonderful and unique. Linnea gives me strength and makes me smile. She is strong, and yet needs my strength. To me, Linnea has an incredible beauty, no one compares. Linnea is my world."

Mike's tension evaporated as the words flowed out. Amy could feel the love and devotion pouring out. Amy was speechless. Seeing this, Mike continued.

"This is why I can't back down. I must protect her. I must protect every person's ability to love someone the way I do. Life deserves that much. The World Military doesn't seem to agree. Personal opinion. And that saddens me."

Amy let out the breath she was holding. She said, "I hope for all of our sakes, that you and Chris get your wish and dream. I'm rooting for you."

"I know," Mike replied.

**

Gen Willson hugs me and asks, "Does she know about you?"

I say, "Yes."

"Ok, they think I'm here to question you about the soldiers that were killed in Waveport. But I know the truth, y'all need to be careful. They are working on something big."

She smiles. "Good luck, Captain. Be in touch. See ya. Let them go."

We get in the car and head back. Juliet asks, "What was that about?"

I say, "Me and Gen Willson go way back. That was her way to give me a heads up."

Amy says, "I'm confused."

I say, "My military history, that's all."

"Oh, ok good." She smiles.

I whisper to Mike and tell him what she said. The limo stops and the driver lets me and Mike out as we walk out of sight. We teleport back.

Mike says, "Let me know if we have any more press conferences."

He left. I went to the command center, got into my uniform, and flew out to Raven City.

I say, "Captain Arrow to Bird Watch. Do we have anything?"

"No cap, nothing right now."

I land on a roof. It's a very quiet night. I say something big is coming and soon. I sit on the roof and watch over the city for a few hours.

I fly back. I land in the command center. I go to pick Karley up and Tiff opens the door. I hear a man ask, "Who is it?" as I see Kevin. I come through the door. As I grab him, I hit him, he falls into the wall. He comes at me. I flip him through the table.

I say, "I didn't come to fight, but tonight I'm up for anything."

Tiff says, "Now I got to take care of him."

I pick Karley up and leave as Tiff says, "Chris, it isn't what you think it is."

I put Karley to bed. I go get a shower. I get out and start drinking. Hanna comes in and takes the glass out of my hand. She says I heard it happened again. I grab her hand as I stand up.

**

Returning back to the apartment, Mike found Linnea and hugged her tightly. Mike whispered to her, "I never want to let you go. I love you!"

Linnea said, "I love you, too! Are you okay?"

Mike replied, "Never better."

They made love right there in the living room.

Mike said, "I have to work tonight. I need to keep you safe."

Linnea said, "I know you do."

Mike got up and took a shower, grabbed an energy drink and called Tommy.

"Hello?" Tommy answered.

"Tommy, this is Mike. How are you feeling tonight? Up to work?" Mike replied.

Tommy said, "I'm always up to working. Think it will be like last time?"

"I do. I don't know what is going on, but something big is brewing. Our families will never be safe if we don't figure it out. Meet me at 7 pm tonight. Get a good dinner, because I plan on working late tonight," Mike said.

"Sounds good," Tommy sighed. Tommy knew they might burn out if they kept this pace up, but he also knew they needed to do this.

Mike spent the evening relaxing. Linnea and Mike worked

together to cook dinner. They had pork chops and potato salad. Linnea and Mike savored every bite. Soon, Mike got up and kissed Linnea goodbye. Then, Mike got ready and went to meet Tommy at the SUV.

**

Tiff helps Kevin up. She says, "Sorry," and kisses him. "It's more than he knows."

**

Hanna turns as I stood up. She looks up at me as I pull her close and kiss her. She smiles. As Karley screams. Me and Hanna run to Karley. I pick her up as she cries.

She says, "Daddy, maw maw and paw paw are in trouble, they need you now."

Hanna says, "Go, I have her."

I teleport out and get my uniform. I fly out. Bird Watch says, "I'm with you, cap."

I land. I hear yelling. I see no cops. I see US military as I see flashes and hear gun shots. As lights hit me and they swarm me. I see Wayne, Billy and Travis. Wayne takes off as the other two and the unit who just executed my family. I scream "No" as I ran and shot arrows into the soldiers. As I break Billy's neck then stomp his head in.

Travis backs up as I put arrows through his knees he falls and screams in pain. I grab an arrow and put it through the base of his skull as I run to the two bodies and see there my mom and dad. I go in the house and kill the soldiers in the house and see my brother and sister is safe. I fly out as the cops show up and the news vans swarm. I land in a field as I cry and my phone rings and its Detective Juliet.

**

Tiff and Kevin sees the news and says, "Oh my goodness." Hanna sees it and starts to cry.

**

I put on my suit and tie and show up at the crime scene. I see

Wesley and Bella as they cry and hug me.

I whispered, "I am so sorry, I tried to save them."

The media swarms us. They ask, "What are you going to do, Mr. Stamper?"

I say, "Get justice!"

As we leave, I get us away and teleport them to the base. We go into my apartment. It's really late. I tell them they can share the guest room for the night.

**

Blue Hurricane and Waterspout drove into Waveport City, idly chatting about life, the universe and everything else. Talking just to pass the time. Soon, they arrived in the city.

"Lighthouse, this is Blue Hurricane. We've just arrived at Waveport. Beginning to drive around," Blue Hurricane said into his mic."

"All is quiet out there. In all four cities, for that matter. But I will keep you posted," Lighthouse responded.

"It's like all the crooks took the day off," Waterspout muttered.

Blue Hurricane glanced at him. "Spooky, isn't it?"

Just then, a woman ran into the street, waving her arms. "Help me!" the woman shouted.

Waterspout slammed on the brakes and swerved the car to narrowly miss her. She ran up to the car and jumped in the backseat, yelling, "Go! Go! Go!"

"What is going on, miss?" Blue Hurricane asked, turning to her.

"My husband is trying to kill me. Please help me and get me outta here!"

Nodding to Waterspout.

"Alright, where to?" Hurricane asked.

The lady, Lorraine they would discover, gave them the address to her sister's house. They talked about what she would do, she concluded that she would call the police as soon as she arrived.

The rest of the night was without incident and they each went home exhausted.

CHAPTER SIXTEEN

I get Karley dressed. Hanna gets in a black dress as I put on my class A uniform. Everyone meets in the vehicle bay as we leave early morning before daylight. I tell my men to, "Keep your eyes out, take anyone out that is military."

The funeral starts as the whole city watches the convoy of law enforcement. Also, state and city government officials and the other three Mayors.

With our vehicles behind the hearse, I tell Bird Watch, Dead Watch, Over Watch and Lighthouse to watch our backs. The funeral went without a problem as we made it to the base without being detected.

Karley says, "Uncles and Aunt Bell I love y'all."

Tiff comes and knocks on the door. I open it. She comes in and sits down.

Tiff says, "I know you don't want to see me and your mad and hurt. I just want to say I'm sorry about your mom and dad."

I give Wes and Bella their apartment right next door. A few days later, the news announces the election winners. Elected governor is Amy Nielson, Raven City Mayor is Chris Stamper, Opoulus city Mayor Zach Johnson, Mark City Mayor Tony Tyler and Waveport City Mayor Eli Watson. Everyone claps as they cheer and ready for a new free life. Hanna throws her arms around my neck and kisses me in front of everyone.

She blushes and smiles shyly. She whispers, "You kissed me first."

I kiss her back and I laugh. I say, "See, it's ok." I congratulate Mike and I thank everyone in the base who helped. My phone rings and Amy says, "We need to celebrate, Mayor Stamper. Let's all go out."

Tiff says, "Congrats Chris and Mike. And I will take the kids tonight."

I tell Tiff, "Thank you and congrats on you and Kevin you will have y'alls freedom."

I tell Mike, "Get your wife and let's go celebrate with Gov Nielson and Det Nielson." I ask Hanna to be my date tonight.

**

Mike sat watching the election coverage on the news for the first time in his life. Linnea sat next to him. Both waited for the results, already knowing what it would be, but still expecting the worst. The tallies poured in slowly, much slower than hoped for. Finally, Mike's breath hitched as they announced it. Quad Cities News Network said the words they all expected: "Raven City Mayor is Chris Stamper."

Mike and Linnea were hugging and kissing as Chris texted his congratulations. Mike texted back, "Congrats. I will be there with Linnea."

Mike said, "Here's to a normal life. I love you, babe."

Mike took his time selecting his celebratory outfit, from his Doc. Martin's to his tie, every thread he wore was hand chosen to stand out. Then he chose a light cologne to go with his mood.

Linnea took her time as well. She chose a form fitting dress that was a shimmering black with a matte black scarf to hang off her bare shoulders. Linnea's perfume accented Mike's cologne. The effect of both of them was being ready for a new type of battle, battle in the diplomatic arena. They left the apartment, dressed to impress and ready for anything.

**

Hanna says, "Of course, I accept."

She goes gets dressed as the four of us go to meet the Mayor's limo. The driver opens the door and says, "Congratulations, Mr. Mayor."

As we get in, he shuts the door. We pull up to a fancy restaurant. The driver lets us out. I take Hanna's hand and Mike takes Linnea's hand. We see Amy and Juliet. They wave us over. The women introduce themselves as the women talk.

I zone out as the ship wrecked on the island as we all stood on the shore as arrows started flying at us. I feel Hanna touch my hand.

She asks, "Are you ok?"

I smile. I say, "Yes."

She looks at me. "Amy was saying something to you."

I look at Amy. I say, Sorry." She smiles.

"It's ok. I was just saying I will show you everything."

I say, "Thank you."

She perks up and says, "I can't wait until we're sworn in!"

Juliet says, "This is great, I can't wait until that day either."

Juliet asks Hanna, "So, are you two together?"

Hanna looks at me and says, "It's a long story."

Juliet sees the look on my face when she asks, "What about your wife?"

She says, "Sorry, I didn't know. It's still fresh, right?"

I say "Yes, it is."

Mike says, "We won! Let's have fun! A round on me."

He takes Linnea's hand and they go to the dance floor. I take Hanna's and I pull her close. I see two guys ask Amy and Juliet to dance. I ask Hanna, "What's in it for you to be with me?"

She looks at me shocked and a little hurt. "There's nothing in it for me besides my heart, Chris, what makes you think that?"

I say, "Well look at all that's happened to me. You can have a normal life."

She says, "Tiff wants that, I want this life with you."
**

Mike and Linnea swayed somewhat in time to the music. More enjoying each other's company than dancing, as neither was very coordinated. Mike enjoyed the smell of Linnea's perfume and breathed in deeply.

"You look wonderful tonight, Mrs. Smith. We don't do this enough," Mike said.

Linnea replied, "You're right, Mr. Smith. We don't. Mike, let's have a kid! I want children."

Mike grinned ear-to-ear. "Yes, let's! We need that in our life. I love you so much!"

Linnea was taken aback by how quickly Mike agreed. She knew it would mean even more to balance in the already hectic life Mike lived, but Linnea knew how truthful Mike had been.

As the song wound down, Mike and Linnea left the dance floor to get drinks. Mike got a Long Island iced tea and Linnea got a Tropical Doc Holliday. In between long sips of drinks, they kissed deeply. Linnea and Mike's conversation never ceasing. They talked about everything they hadn't had a chance to lately with Mike's work, from science to favorite baby names. The last turning into a small debate that ranged from biblical names, like Selah and Elam, to more mainstream, like Bart and Summer.
**

Hanna says, "Chris, even if we were normal or not, my life is with you. That's all I really want, is your heart."

As I feel her arms tighten around the back of my neck. She buries her head into my chest, then our eyes meet as she looks up. I kiss her. She looks surprised as she kisses back. As we dance, I see the spark in her green eyes.

I smile as I see everyone laughing and having fun. Hanna smiles and asks, "What?"

I say, "This is nice. Everyone is having fun and laughing. I haven't seen that in a long time."

As the cameras started flashing as the reporters come in. I spin Hanna around and bend her back then kiss Hanna then bring her up. I see Amy and Juliet give them phone numbers to the men they were with. I look at Mike and Linnea.

I say, "They are the two who know what true love is. You can see it in their eyes when they look at each other."

Hanna asks, "Do we look like that?"

I look at her. "It doesn't matter what others see or thinks, it's how we feel. It's where our hearts are is what matters." She smiles.

Right then I knew, I see it in her eyes as we danced as the music played. We held each other close.

Amy comes up. "Let's go, too many people and reporters," as I say, "Mike, let's go."

We all get through the crowd and get in the limo everyone laughs as I ask, "Is everyone in?" I smile.

Mike says, "This has been the most normal fun we have had in a while. I want more days like this."

Hanna puts her head on my shoulder and says, "Me too."

We drop off Amy and Juliet, then the driver drops us off at my family home. We go in the house then teleport back to the base as I tell Mike and Linnea, "Goodnight."

**

Tiff and Kevin are talking. Tiff says, "We will tell Chris tonight, ok?"

**

Mike and Linnea arrive back at their apartment, slightly buzzed and wrapped in each other's arms. As soon as the door opened, they kissed each other with passionate fury. The door was barely shut when they were making love. Hours later, they lay in a crumpled heap in bed, still panting and exhausted. Soon after, both Mike and Linnea were asleep in each other's arms.

The next morning, Mike woke up. A mild throbbing headache touched his temples. Caffeine. Mike needed caffeine. He got up and went into the fridge, got two energy drinks and chugged the first.

Mike's thoughts turned to how blissfully normal their lives were the night before. A smile graced his face as he did.

"Could I really live a normal life?" Mike questioned himself out loud.

Linnea, having crept up behind him, answered, "Yes, we really can!"

Mike spun, startled, and said, "Hello you! How'd you sleep?"

Linnea said, "Great. Thanks to you."

They embraced and kissed.

Mike said, "Unfortunately, time to get started with the day."

Mike made breakfast, took a shower, and got dressed in a suit. He went to the command center to check on things after that.

CHAPTER SEVENTEEN

Hanna unlocks our door. As the door shuts behind us, there's a knock. Hanna answers the door. As she opens the door, she sees Tiff and Kevin.

Tiff says, "Sorry, but we need to talk to Chris."

Hanna looks at Kevin's face and says, "That might be a bad idea."

I come to the door. I say to Kevin, "So you're stupid, you didn't learn."

Kevin says, "Please, can we talk, it's very serious."

I get a dip. Hanna lets them in. They sit down.

Kevin says, "Please, just listen to me, Captain, and let me finish before you talk. Well, I made it look like something was going on between me and Tiff. She came to me to surprise you on the day you got sworn in as Mayor. That's it. I did that to get her, now she's mine, and I really am in love with her. Because of her, I'm telling you this. We never did anything sexually or anything until now that we're together."

"I also gave Bessie a mixed blood samples from all of you guys so they can use it. All I know is it's going to happen when you get sworn in. I'm sorry, Captain, I never wanted to hurt anyone. I just wanted you out of the way."

Tiff looks at Hanna and says, "Treat him right, it's ok for you to be with him."

We hear a scream from next door at Wesley's, so we run over. We run in and I pick Karley up. She cries, "Daddy!"

Karley says, "A lot of people are fixing to get hurt. I seen people everywhere in parts."

I hold her until she falls asleep. I put her in her bed. I tell Kevin and Tiff to, "Get an idea of what they are going to do or how they are going to use the mutated blood."

Kevin says, "Ok, no problem. Will be done, boss."

As they leave, Hanna says, "There goes the fun and Tiff gave me her blessing to be with you."

She still has that tight, black dress on as she walks up to me and throws her arms around my neck.

**

Mike sat in the command center for an hour, hoping for something to do, but glad for the boredom. He spent the time reminiscing over the night before. At the same time, Mike thought that things must be coming to a head. How much more would the World Military throw at them? Time would only tell.

Mike got up abruptly, still sipping his energy drink. Mike walked back to the apartment and began to text Amy. Linnea came over to see what he was doing.

He texted, "What should I be doing right now as Chief of Staff?"

Amy texted back, "This is a surprise. I didn't expect you to try and start right away. You should probably set up a meeting with the incoming staff and start prepping all you need for day one."

Mike replied, "Ok. That makes sense, thanks."

Mike knew that the command center had a list of the upcoming staff with phone numbers and e-mails.

Amy replied, "No worried, any time."

Mike went back to the command center and made a copy of the staff list. Then went back to the apartment to begin setting up a meeting for that day, if everyone could make it. Mike followed that up with a text to make sure everyone saw it. Then, he waited.

**

Hanna smiles as she kisses me. I sit her on the counter as she unbuttons my suit jacket. She pulls my tie off, then my button up, white collared shirt off. I pick her up and carry her to my bedroom as she undresses her black dress and it falls to the floor. As we kiss and make love we connect as her one and permanent mate. She in laying on me. She smiles. Her long brown hair is a mess.

She gets up and she puts on some tight jeans and one of my t-shirts on. She says I'm going to cook. She kisses me. I pull her back into the bed as she laughs and says, "Let me go cook."

I go get a shower. I put on normal clothes, I get a dip and go watch TV. I spit in a bottle as the news comes on. Hanna comes in and sits by me. They say, "Governor Nielson and Mayor Stamper all celebrated their victory."

The news anchor says, "Look at the love between the Mayor and the woman he's with. Look at the love and smiles. With that kind of love and friendship they have, I'm confident our cities will be safe."

Hanna smiles. "See, they see it, too, but you haven't asked me to be your girl."

I say, "Look on your chest."

She sees the arrow symbol brand on her chest. She smiles.

I say, "Will you be my girl?"

She says, "Of course."

We fall asleep on the couch together. She falls asleep on my chest. I wake up to Karley and Hanna playing while Hanna made breakfast. I kiss Hanna as she puts her arms around my neck.

She says, "Good morning."

I say, "Good morning. I'm working tonight."

She smiles. "Ok, that's fine. I will come, too."

Hanna hands me my plate. We eat. I have the day off from being Mayor. I kiss Karley on the head. She giggled as Hanna let her down to play. We sit and watch cartoons with Karley then Jr came in. He sits down beside Hanna and they start joking. I see a change in his eyes.

**

Mike sat impatiently waiting for replies. The television held no interest and he sat tapping his foot. Mike kept reminding himself that the other staff members had lives, too, but that didn't alleviate the gnawing need to do something. Finally, after an hour, the first text came back, simply stating, "You're on."

Mike sighed heavily in relief. Like a small fire, the texts poured in. And like that, Mike set up the first meeting. Mike set the meeting for 3 pm with a simple agenda. The meeting would serve to answer one question: How can each staff member help to hit the ground running?

As the hour approached, the only staff member not to respond is the secretary, Hanna. This suited Mike just fine. He supposed that they (Hanna and Chris) were still celebrating.

Soon, Mike stood in the Mayor's conference room. As the staff members filtered in, Mike greeted each by name. They spent the first 15 minutes getting to know each other and the rest of the 45 minutes solidifying what day one would look like. At the end of the meeting, the staff had a clear picture of what they would tell Chris on day one.

**

We go to the command center after dropping the kids off to Tiff and Kevin. We get our uniforms on and fly out together.

She says, "This is fun."

We land on the tallest building in Raven City and perch on the ledge. I hear people land behind us say, "Hey Captain and Emerald Arrow." We turn to see Red Web and Shadow.

I hear a scream coming up from two blocks up. We run and dive off of the building. We get to the alley. We see a lot of World Military trying to hurt a woman as we run down. I shot arrows. I hit and kill several soldiers. So did Emerald. Red Web and Shadow webbed them up. Emerald puts the woman behind her to protect her. As we fight and kill, I hear, "Do it now!" I hear a scream, then I see Emerald fall.

I run and catch her as she fell. I see the woman Emerald was protecting catch fire and run screaming. I hold Hanna in my arms. I see blood. I see a knife laying on the ground. I hit my radio.

I say, "Bird Watch."

I hear, "Go ahead, Captain Arrow."

I say, "Get Lt. Bass ready. Emerald Arrow is down. She was stabbed in the back by a knife."

Red Web yells, "Get Emerald out of here, Captain, we got them."

I teleport her back in my arms. Holly had a stretcher ready as I lay Hanna on it. Holly says, "Trust me. Go and help Red Web and Shadow."

I teleport back. I see they are pinned down as I run and shoot arrows into the soldiers. As they turn, I hit them with super strength and throw a dumpster. I kill twenty with a dumpster and trapped one. Red Web uses super strength and kills the last of them. It gets quiet, so I teleport home. I walk in to the waiting room of the med bay.

**

After the meeting, Mike goes back to the apartment to celebrate his success with Linnea. Mike rushes in the apartment door and up to her to hug and kiss her.

Linnea said, "Someone had a good day."

"Who, me?" Mike replied with mock surprise. He continued. "Yeah, it went really well. The staff is really working well together."

Linnea responded, "That's good. Are you hungry? I'm making dinner soon."

"Starving!" Mike said.

They ate dinner as Mike mentally prepared to go out tonight working. As they ate, idle talk filled the air.

Mike messaged Tommy to get ready, tonight they would go out. Tommy responded, "Ok." They met up and drove to Waveport City. Blue Hurricane and Waterspout immediately got a call to respond to a fire at a building. Blue Hurricane approached the Fire Marshall and said, "Is there anyone inside? I can stop this thing quickly if no one is in there."

The Marshall said, "As far as we know, the building is clear."

Blue Hurricane began to concentrate and sucked all the oxygen from around the building, immediately dousing the flames.

The Fire Marshall, impressed, said, "Thanks," and shook Blue Hurricane's hand.

**

As I sat down, I pull my hood back and I waited while Hanna is in the OR. Tyson comes in and sits beside me. I put my head in my hands.

Tyson says, "You can't protect everyone. You have a team, trust them. You, Hanna, everyone here are fighting and willing to give their lives for our freedom and a normal life. Hanna will be OK. She's strong. You won't keep her out of the field with you, Cap. She loves you."

Tiff, Kevin, Jr and Karley come in. Kevin kisses Tiff and looks at me.

Kevin says, "This is horrible what they are doing to make up for the wrong I have done to you. I want to go help her with your permission, Captain."

I say, "Go and help."

He goes straight back. They come hug me. I tell Bird Watch to let all the other be aware of the World Military.

They are everywhere and using all they can to ambush us and let's all watch each other's backs out there. Jacob, Sammy and Skyler come in and ask, "How is Hanna?"

"There is no news yet."

We're waiting, so we all wait. Holly comes out.

"Hanna made it through the surgery just fine. We won't know if she can walk until she wakes up if she can it's because of Kevin."

"The blade went through close to her spine but it did damage to her spine and nerves. Kevin repaired the damage the best he could. He did better than I could have. You can go back and wait for her to wake up."

Tiff smiles. "Chris go, I will watch the kids tonight."

I hug Tiff, kiss the kids on the head and I go sit by Hanna's bed. I hold her hand as the doctors and nurses come in and out to check on her. I kiss her hand and say, "They will pay for this, I promise," as my phone rings.

I hear, "Mayor Stamper?"

I say, "Go ahead, Governor Nielson.

"We get sworn in three days from now."

**

As mike leaves the scene of the fire, Lighthouse contacts him.

"Lighthouse to Blue Hurricane, come in."

Blue Hurricane responded, "Go ahead, Lighthouse."

"Hurricane, be careful out there. The World Military just hit Captain and Emerald Arrow. Emerald Arrow is down for the count."

Lighthouse's emotions betrayed her concern.

"Thanks for the heads up."

Just then, a crack rang out as a sniper took a shot at them. Luckily, the sniper wasn't good and the shot hit the pavement nearby. Blue Hurricane started to erect a shield as a second shot rang out a split second later.

By this time, Waterspout was moving behind Blue Hurricane. This was Tommy Hale's last mistake. The shield was a split second too late as it grazed Blue Hurricane and entered Waterspout's eye socket. With an explosion of grey and red matter, Tommy Hale went limp.

Next thing Blue Hurricane knew, he was flying at impossible speeds towards the sniper. Using wind and dust, Mike ripped apart the sniper and spotter limb from limb, piece by piece. All that was left when he was done was a dirty, red splotch on the ground.

CHAPTER EIGHTEEN

Hanna wakes up and sees Chris asleep with his hand holding hers and his head on the bed beside her. I wake up to her touching the side of my face. I look up at her. She smiles.

"Good morning, sleepy head."

There's a knock on the door as Holly comes in and checks Hanna's vitals. Holly smiles.

"Looks normal."

As a knock on the door, Kevin comes in, he asks, "Dr. Bass, have you done it yet?"

Dr. Bass says, "Of course not, Dr. Blane, not without you. Let's check now."

He stands back as Dr. Bass says, "Let's check your reflexes," as Dr. Bass pokes Hanna's feet and Hanna says, "Ouch," as her legs move. Holly runs the bottom of the reflex hammer on the bottom of both feet as Hanna giggles. Holly checks her reflex as she taps right on the bottom of the knee on both Hanna's legs. Dr. Bass says her reflexes are strong. I smile at Hanna. I tell Dr.

Blane, "Thank you." Holly whispers in Hanna's ear. I see a big smile as Hanna says, "Thank you both."

Hanna lays back smiling at me. I ask, "What did Dr. Bass whisper to you?" I see the light in her eyes and the glow in her face and skin. She smiles.

Hanna says, "You're going to be a dad again."

I smile and hug her. She smiles.

"You're happy."

I say, "Yes, I am. We're having a baby together."

I kiss her. She smiles as I tell her to get some rest.

We kiss. She closes her eyes and I say, "I love you."

She says, "I love you, too."

Hanna whispers, "I'm going to be there the day you get sworn in. I'm going to support you. I'm not takin' no as an answer and it's not a question."

I smile. "Ok, you can go."

She smiles. "See, I win, my love."

I watch her fall asleep. I get up quietly and head to the command center.

Arial says, "Hey Captain."

I ask, "Are you ready for pay back?"

She smiles. "Of course."

She opens the fly door. I take off and fly into Raven City.
**

Mike stares at the stain that used to be World Military thugs, panting.

"Blue Hurricane to Lighthouse. Waterspout is down. A sniper got him and winged me. Threat is neutralized. I'm brining the remains back to base."

"Umm. Uh, okay. I don't know what to tell Bird Watch or the family," Lighthouse responded, completely shaken.

Blue Hurricane said, steely resolve in his voice, "You get them together and I will tell them. Have doctors Cook and Lake get ready to receive the body."

Blue Hurricane swopped down and picked up Tommy with air. He then flew as fast as he could to base. The doctors were waiting for him and took his body to a makeshift morgue.

Blue Hurricane steeled himself more for the next step: addressing the family. Pulling his mask off, Mike called Lighthouse.

"Is the family together?"

Lighthouse, in between sobs, said, "Yes, they are ready."

Mike went to the conference room they commandeered and immediately began.

"Tommy was brave beyond mention tonight. He did EVERYTHING he was supposed to. Tommy was a friend and my most trusted companion. Tonight, the World Military made it more personal than ever when, instead of targeting me, they took out Tommy in a blood thirsty way. The ones who did it have paid, but I will make the ones responsible suffer. I promise you!"

**

I hear Blue Hurricane, Red Web and Captain Cross say, "We're with you."

I ask, "Are y'all ready to end this tonight?"

I tell Red Web, "To go after Bessie," Captain Cross, "Go find Lin Chi," Blue Hurricane, "Who do you want?"

He says, "I want the Orator."

I say, "Stay where you are. I will give you a lift."

He says, "Ok, Captain."

"You can't get to him easily, so I will fly you in."

"Ok, I copy that Captain I say I'm going to drop you off and go after Pres. Wayne."

I dive down Blue Hurricane reaches up and I grab his arms he grabs mine as we fly high. I say in the mic, "They are all in the Quad City, not far from where we're getting sworn in." I ask, "Are you ready, Blue Hurricane?"

He says, "Yes," as I release him as he dives down. I watch him use his air ability to land quietly and safely.

I fly back up then dive and land on the roof of a different

hotel. Bird Watch says, "He's in room 1140."

I teleport into his room as Bird Watch says, "Be careful, they know you guys might come."

I see Wayne, he turns, "Well, what a surprised! I wasn't expecting you, Captain Arrow! Wow!" as soldiers moved in, guns drawn on me.

He laughs, "I got you!" as he says, "You're under arrest," as they go to grab me their hands go through me. Wayne yells, "What, where is he?" as they heard sounds of arrows in the air. As Wayne sees everyone fall around him. He sees an arrow in the wall. He goes to say, "You missed," but can't talk.

I say, "This is what you deserved for what you did to my family, friends, my city, my country. President Wayne, you have failed our country," as he falls to the floor in a puddle of blood where the arrow went through his neck.

**

Blue Hurricane creeps along the top of the roof with his shield up. Blue Hurricane is careful not to draw the fire of the soldiers on the tops of the other roofs. The door to down below is guarded by two shotgun-wielding soldiers. Blue Hurricane removes the air from around them and they wordlessly go down. Working quickly, Blue Hurricane rushes silently though the, hopefully, not alarmed door.

"Hurricane to Lighthouse, I'm in. Where is this bastard?" he whispered into his mic.

"Looks like he is in room 1417. Be careful," Lighthouse responded.

Blue Hurricane responded, "I will. 10-4."

He proceeded down the steps to the 15th floor.

As Blue Hurricane slowly cracked open the door, he heard a radio go off on a soldier saying, "Heads up, Z, he's on his way to you. Looks like Blue Hurricane."

With that, Mike burst through the door and sent a big blast of air towards the sound. A single shot rang out, deflected by the shield.

The shot was like kicking a hornet's nest. Soldier must have commandeered the floor, because door after door opened up. They threatened to overwhelm Blue Hurricane as they pour out of the doors. Just as all seems lost, Blue Hurricane lets loose a hurricane force blast of wind, killing all of them and shattering the doors.

CHAPTER NINETEEN

He lays at me feet. I put an arrow in his head as I say, "Complete Bird Watch."

She says, "Copy, Captain Arrow."

I hear people outside the door as they breached, I shot arrows. I teleport out as far as I could.

Bird Watch says, "Captain, don't fly, they are looking in the sky."

I say, "Thank you, Bird Watch. I copy," as I teleport.

As I run, I ask for an update, she says, "Blue Hurricane is still on his mission. Captain Cross is still looking for Yang. No luck so far. Captain Arrow, the death of the president has spread. The world and US military is on alert."

I say, "I will distract them. So Blue Hurricane can complete his task."

I fly and land in front of the Orator's hotel as the guns point at me as they shoot. I reflected the bullets with telekinesis as I reach them and shoot arrows. I use telekinesis to throw them. I hear a scream behind me as I see a sniper hanging from a web.

Red Web says, "Got your back, Captain," as he shoots web as we fight.

"Overwatch to Captain Arrow."

I say, "Go ahead."

"Captain Cross says he's going to keep searching for Yang."

I say, "Copy," as I kill a few more soldiers.

Red Web hits them as I use the super strength. As we fight, Red Web says, "I'm tiring out," as he takes cover.

I say, "Me too, but get your second wind. We have to keep going for Blue Hurricane."

Red Web stands up. Shadow comes in shooting. I cover Shadow as we make progress in. I say, "Y'all are well trained."

Red Web says, "Well, Captain, you trained us," as he laughs. As we continue to shoot and use our abilities to kill.

**

Blue Hurricane sped down the next flight of stairs as fast as he could manage. Using a directed blast of air, he blew the door clean off its hinges. The door flew into a soldier and crushed him against the wall.

Blue Hurricane burst into the hallway with debris floating behind him. As the soldiers fired upon him, Blue Hurricane deflected bullets left and right, sending debris through five and six soldiers. Yells of anguish and pain rang out as soldiers were disabled and died on either side of him.

Desperation began to mount as the soldiers realized that were on the losing team. So, someone threw a grenade.

Blue Hurricane, with adrenaline pumping, saw the grenade fly in slow motion towards him and blew it right back to sender. The sound of the explosion was deafening in such a small hallway. At least ten soldiers were scattered to bits. The remaining five soldiers were too injured or shell-shocked to move. Blue Hurricane touched the ground. The only sound inside the hallway was the groans of the dying.

"Idiots!" Blue Hurricane exclaimed.

He then proceeded to walk to room 1417. It was time to end this. Time to stop the mastermind, time to kill the Orator.

At the threshold, Blue Hurricane tried again to blow the door off its hinges. This time, it bounced off a barricade set up within the large suite. Immediately, two flame throwers fired out of the hold. Luckily for Blue Hurricane, his shield wind redirected the flames, the fire singed the edges of his suit. Picking up some debris with wind, Hurricane flung them at the tanks of each flamethrower, causing them to explode. Silence reigned. Then, out of the smokey room, Blue Hurricane was addressed.

"Well, well, well. Only one of you? Long time no see, Mike. I figured out who you are just in time for tonight."

"Too late then, I'm afraid. Tonight, you're finished," Blue Hurricane responded, sending a gust of wind into the smoke.

As the smoke cleared, he could see the Orators arm.

The Orator ran at Mike in response, ignoring his pain. Just as he started, Blue Hurricane flung a chunk of two-by-four at the Orator's head. The chunk hit with a resounding crack, knocking him off his feet. Mike walked up to the Orator and checked his pulse. The Orator was dead. It was finally over.

**

I hear Blue Hurricane say over the headset, "This mission is complete, the Orator is dead."

I say, "Copy that, Blue Hurricane, we are getting out of here, are you free and clear?"

I hear, "Yes, Captain, I am You guys get out of there."

I say Red Web Shadow "Teleport out of here, I will cover you."

Red Web grabs Shadow, they teleport. I get and take cover then teleport out of there as I made it back to command center.

I hear silence. I look around. Everyone is watching the TV. I pull my hood back. I walk up and see the news on. I stand quietly behind Arial as the reporters show the hotels, police and military. They show the body bags as the reporters say, "It's been confirmed. The President and the World Leader have been assassinated and confirmed dead. Evidence shows the vigilantes did this. We will update you as more develops. Goodnight."

As everyone cheered and clapped, they celebrated as Mike hands me a beer.

He says, "Here's to a normal life, finally!" as I agree and drink it down.

I say, "I need to go see Hanna. I'm going to be a father again."

Mike says, "Then what are you doing talking to me, go to her!"

I run out and down to med bay I go into Hanna's room and she's gone. Someone passes by as I come out in the hallway a nurse says, "Oh, Captain."

I ask, "Where is Hanna?"

The nurse smiles. "They moved her and Dr. Holly is with her."

I take off running. I open my apartment door. I see Tiff, Kevin, Holly, Jr, Karley and Hanna. Karley screams, "Daddy!" as she runs. I pick her up as Hanna hugs me.

Hanna kisses me and says, "Y'all did it, and no one got hurt."

Kevin and Tiff clapped and I told Kevin, "Thank you."

He said, "It was nothing. We have our freedom now."

I said, "Yes, finally, we do. Kevin, you're part of the family."

He smiles. Tiff kisses him. Jr says, "Dad, you were awesome out there!"

I hug him. I say, "A normal life, what's that, it's going to be strange not living underground."

As everyone left, we were in bed. Hanna whispers, "Thank you for a normal life." We kiss and fall asleep.

CHAPTER TWENTY

A couple days has passed. I cook breakfast and bring it to Hanna. I help her sit up. She eats. I kiss her and go get a shower. I put my suit and tie on. Hanna smiles you clean up nice I help her up. She gets dressed. She has her long brown hair down. She has on a long green sun dress. Hanna comes out of our bedroom. I stop and stare.

She smiles. "What?"

I say, "You look beautiful."

She says, "I will look the best that I can for you and today is your day."

She kisses me. I kiss Karley on the head and say, "You look beautiful, too."

We get in the limo and we go pick up Mike and Linnea at their new house in Waveport. We pick up Dr. Bass and her boyfriend, Dr. Miyers, in Raven City. We pick everyone up and the driver says, "Get comfortable with police escort it will be very backed up with traffic."

I ask Mike and Linnea if they settled into their new home. I say, "At least we only work at the old base and don't live there anymore."

Holly smiles and says, "I'm the Mayor's personal doctor."

I laugh and say, "What's new? You have been our doctor for years!"

Rodger Miyers says, "I know what you, friend, and family are. Before you say anything Mayor Stamper, I want to thank y'all for all you do and all you guys have done."

"I also want you to know all of you guys have a special wing in the hospital where all your doctors and nurses all work now. It protects all of the super humans and your family. Also, no one knows about it or about any of you."

I say, "If Holly trusts you, so do I."

He smiles. "I'm glad to help the real heroes and good guys."

We get to the hotel and see Amy, Juliet and their boyfriends. I hear Captain Cross say, "Captain Arrow, still no luck, but I'm closing in on Yang's whereabouts."

**

An hour earlier.

Mike and Linnea check into their hotel room.

"I can't believe we get to stay at a hotel as nice as this," Linnea says.

"Stick with me and we'll go places," Mike says.

The shock of a normal house and a normal life was still very real to them. Their new house was situated along the waterfront with an oceanic view. Mike loved the salt air and loved not living on a base.

Linnea loved having her husband to herself for the past few days, and loved being attached to his hip. Their lives couldn't get better. They spent the last few days making love during the day, unpacking at night and playing video games in the morning.

With the swearing in looming over them, this would change slightly. Mike would be busy for a bit. Normal here they come. The day before, Mike sent out a text to all staff saying simply,

"Are we ready?"

Hanna replied, "We've been ready!"

This echoed the sentiments of the rest of the staff. Mike replied, "Let's do this then."

And now, here they were, getting ready for this momentous occasion. This occasion earned through blood, sweat and tears. The one earned on the backs of fallen comrades. This is for the Tommy's out there and the Hunters, time to change the world.

**

We pull up the driver says, "We will be waiting a while, Mr. Mayor."

I say, "Call me Chris. Ok, thank you for the update."

He says, "Yes sir."

Hanna snuggles up to me and smiles. She says, "I'm so happy and the family home looks so beautiful."

I say, "At least we get a normal life. It's because all the heroes were fighting for it. I wanted this for our kids."

Amy says, "I want to make this state and schools for our super humans I want what is best for all lives here."

I smile. "Of course, governor. As Mayor I will push for that. All lives in every city matter to me also."

Amy says, "Let's do it."

I say, "Ight lets," as the car stops.

The driver gets out as security comes up the driver opens the door.

I step out of the car. I have Hanna take my hand and I pick up Karley as everyone else gets out. Mike gets out with Linnea.

Mike says, "I set up a staff meeting for the transition into office."

I say, "Thank you, and good work."

He says, "No problem."

As the pictures are being taken, we walk into the building.

I say, 'Wow, it's big and open. A lot of people can fit in here," as the reporters line up ready.

I tell Mike, "The first meeting went really great and to keep up the good work."

Amy runs up and says, "Chris, let's go, it's time."

Hanna kisses me and says, "Go get 'em."

I watch Amy get sworn in as governor. Then the other three Mayors got sworn in then they called me up. I took my oath and got sworn in. Then came the chiefs of all police departments as they finished.

I hear Captain Cross say, "I found her, she's in the building."

I yell to Mike, "Go get our families out of here, she's in the building."

I run to Amy, Juliet, Hanna, Karley, as I run on the stage.
**

Captain Cross sees her in the rafters. He yells, "Yang, don't do it. It ain't worth it."

She says, "Too late," as she holds and presses the button.

As the nuclear reactor flashed and shot up in the sky as the clouds turned black. The building shakes as a rafter falls a masked individual came up behind Yang as she turned the blades sliced her up. The rafter fell and Captain Cross dodged it then he fell back and went directly into a broken rafter.

As Yang's body fell in pieces to the ground, Captain Cross looks down and sees the rafter impaled him. He sees the masked man who helped him say, "Sorry, I can't save you." Captain Cross looks at him and spits blood as everything goes black. He says sorry you can rest as he bends down and closes Captain Cross' eyes.
**

As I run, I hear screams. I see a glimpse of Mike running to Linnea and the others. I grabbed Karley, Hanna, Amy and Juliet as I put them in a corner all together. As the building collapses, I see a flash as the reactor explodes with heat, radiation, and blood falls from the sky. As I protect them with my body, a piece of support beam hits me. I hear screams as I black out.

ACKNOWLEDGEMENTS

Christopher Stamper

I would love to thank my family for their love and support and believing in me. I want to thank my co-author for all his hard work and also fixing my spelling and punctuation errors. I know it was aggravating. I couldn't have done it without you. I would like to thank the team at Cadmus Publishing, my author liaison/ agent, Frank Reuter, the editors, and the artist who did the book cover. Thank you all. I also want to thank my high school English teacher, Ms. Everest, who I quote, "You have an amazing imagination to be a writer, but you can't spell or punctuate properly." And, of course, thank you God and our readers and fans.

Michael McCarron

I would like to thank my family and friends for the support given me. I would like to thank Chris for this opportunity. Thanks to our publisher for his support. And finally, but most importantly, thanks to the readers…without you, this means nothing.

ABOUT THE AUTHORS

AUTHOR

My name is Christopher Stamper. I'm 29 years-old. I was born in West Monroe, Louisiana on February 24, 1992. I'm in prison fighting for my freedom and changing a lot in my life with people and my career. I have kids and I'm engaged. I have learned who my friends and family are through this experience. I met my best friend and co-author through this. I'm a back-woods country boy. I have done and accomplished a lot in my life. Now I'm terminally ill, so, I got into writing because a lot of people in my life told me I have a talent in writing and I have the imagination to be an amazing writer, but I can't spell or punctuate properly. So, I hope you enjoy this book series and enjoy every book series we write.

CO-AUTHOR

Mike McCarron was born on December 28th and is 36 years-old He is married to Linnea and together they have a Pomeranian Chihuahua mix dog named Roxxy. I met Chris through a shared experience and we keep each other sane...mostly. He got me writing and editing what we wrote. I hope you enjoy the book series and enjoy our work.

www.ingramcontent.com/pod-product-compliance
Lightning Source LLC
Chambersburg PA
CBHW060555100726
47907CB00005B/1372